~ This book is for doctors everywhere ~

Find out more about Roald Dahl by visiting the website at
roalddahl.com

PUFFIN BOOKS

Published by the Penguin Group
Penguin Books Ltd, 80 Strand, London WC2R 0RL, England
Penguin Group (USA) Inc., 375 Hudson Street, New York, New York 10014, USA
Penguin Group (Canada), 90 Eglinton Avenue East, Suite 700, Toronto, Ontario, Canada M4P 2Y3
(a division of Pearson Penguin Canada Inc.)
Penguin Ireland, 25 St Stephen's Green, Dublin 2, Ireland (a division of Penguin Books Ltd)
Penguin Group (Australia), 250 Camberwell Road, Camberwell, Victoria 3124, Australia
(a division of Pearson Australia Group Pty Ltd)
Penguin Books India Pvt Ltd, 11 Community Centre, Panchsheel Park, New Delhi – 110 017, India
Penguin Group (NZ), 67 Apollo Drive, Rosedale, Auckland 0632, New Zealand
(a division of Pearson New Zealand Ltd)
Penguin Books (South Africa) (Pty) Ltd, 24 Sturdee Avenue, Rosebank, Johannesburg 2196, South Africa

Penguin Books Ltd, Registered Offices: 80 Strand, London WC2R 0RL, England

puffinbooks.com

First published by Jonathan Cape Ltd 1981
Published in Puffin Books 1982
This colour edition published 2011
001 – 10 9 8 7 6 5 4 3 2 1

Text copyright © Roald Dahl Nominee Ltd, 1981
Illustrations copyright © Quentin Blake, 1981
All rights reserved
Colour treatment by Rupert Van Wyk
The moral right of the author and illustrator has been asserted

Made and printed in China

British Library Cataloguing in Publication Data
A CIP catalogue record for this book is available from the British Library

ISBN: 978–0–141–33558–2

THIS BOOK
BELONGS TO
_____

Roald Dahl

George's Marvellous Medicine

illustrated by Quentin Blake

PUFFIN

CONTENTS

WARNING TO READERS:
Do not try to make George's Marvellous
Medicine yourselves at home.
It could be dangerous.

Chapter One

GRANDMA

'I'm going shopping in the village,' George's mother said to George on Saturday morning. 'So be a good boy and don't get up to mischief.'

This was a silly thing to say to a small boy at any time. It immediately made him wonder what sort of mischief he might get up to.

'And don't forget to give Grandma her medicine at eleven o'clock,' the mother said. Then out she went, closing the back door behind her.

Grandma, who was dozing in her chair by the window, opened one wicked little eye and said, 'Now you heard what your mother said, George. Don't forget my medicine.'

'No, Grandma,' George said.

'And just try to behave yourself for once while she's away.'

'Yes, Grandma,' George said.

George was bored to tears. He didn't have a brother or a sister. His father was a farmer and the farm they lived on was miles away from anywhere, so there were never any children to play with. He was tired of staring at pigs and hens and cows and sheep. He was especially tired of having to live in the same house as that grizzly old grunion of a Grandma. Looking after her all by himself was hardly the most exciting way to spend a Saturday morning.

'You can make me a nice cup of tea for a start,' Grandma said to George. 'That'll keep you out of mischief for a few minutes.'

'Yes, Grandma,' George said.

George couldn't help disliking Grandma. She was a selfish grumpy old woman. She had pale brown teeth and a small puckered-up mouth like a dog's bottom.

'How much sugar in your tea today, Grandma?' George asked her.

'One spoon,' she said. 'And no milk.'

Most grandmothers are lovely, kind, helpful old ladies, but not this one. She spent all day and every day sitting in her chair by the window, and she was always complaining, grousing, grouching, grumbling, griping about something or other. Never once, even on her best days, had she smiled at George and said, 'Well, how are you this morning, George?' or 'Why don't you and I have a game of Snakes and Ladders?' or 'How was school today?' She didn't seem to care about other people, only about herself. She was a miserable old grouch.

George went into the kitchen and made Grandma a cup of tea with a teabag. He put one spoon of sugar in it and no milk. He stirred the sugar well and carried the cup into the living-room.

Grandma sipped the tea. 'It's not sweet enough,' she said. 'Put more sugar in.'

George took the cup back to the kitchen and added another spoonful of sugar. He stirred it again and carried it carefully in to Grandma.

'Where's the saucer?' she said. 'I won't have a cup without a saucer.'

George fetched her a saucer.

'And what about a teaspoon, if you please?'

'I've stirred it for you, Grandma. I stirred it well.'

'I'll stir my own tea, thank you very much,' she said. 'Fetch me a teaspoon.'

George fetched her a teaspoon.

When George's mother or father were home, Grandma never ordered George about like this. It was only when she had him on her own that she began treating him badly.

'You know what's the matter with you?' the old woman said, staring at George over the rim of the teacup with those bright wicked little eyes. 'You're *growing* too fast. Boys who grow too fast become stupid and lazy.'

'But I can't help it if I'm growing fast, Grandma,' George said.

'Of course you can,' she snapped. 'Growing's a nasty childish habit.'

'But we *have* to grow, Grandma. If we didn't grow, we'd never be grown-ups.'

'Rubbish, boy, rubbish,' she said. 'Look at me. Am I growing? Certainly not.'

'But you did once, Grandma.'

'Only *very little*,' the old woman answered. 'I gave up growing when I was extremely small, along with all the other nasty childish habits like laziness and disobedience and greed and sloppiness and untidiness and stupidity. You haven't given up any of these things, have you?'

'I'm still only a little boy, Grandma.'

'You're eight years old,' she snorted. 'That's old enough to know better. If you don't stop growing soon, it'll be too late.'

'Too late for what, Grandma?'

'It's ridiculous,' she went on. 'You're nearly as tall as me already.'

George took a good look at Grandma. She certainly was a *very tiny* person. Her legs were so short she had to have a footstool to put her feet on, and her head only came halfway up the back of the armchair.

'Daddy says it's fine for a man to be tall,' George said.

'Don't listen to your daddy,' Grandma said. 'Listen to me.'

'But how do I stop myself growing?' George asked her.

'Eat less chocolate,' Grandma said.

'Does chocolate make you grow?'

'It makes you grow the *wrong way*,' she snapped. 'Up instead of down.'

Grandma sipped some tea but never took her eyes from the little boy who stood before her. 'Never grow up,' she said. 'Always down.'

'Yes, Grandma.'

'And stop eating chocolate. Eat cabbage instead.'

'Cabbage! Oh no, I don't like cabbage,' George said.

'It's not what you like or what you don't like,' Grandma snapped. 'It's what's good for you that counts. From now on, you must eat cabbage three times a day. Mountains of cabbage! And if it's got caterpillars in it, so much the better!'

'Owch,' George said.

'Caterpillars give you brains,' the old woman said.

'Mummy washes them down the sink,' George said.

'Mummy's as stupid as you are,' Grandma said. 'Cabbage doesn't taste of anything without a few boiled caterpillars in it. Slugs, too.'

'Not *slugs*!' George cried out. 'I couldn't eat slugs!'

'Whenever I see a live slug on a piece of lettuce,' Grandma said, 'I gobble it up quick before it crawls away. Delicious.' She squeezed her lips together tight so that her mouth became a tiny wrinkled hole. 'Delicious,' she said again. 'Worms and slugs and beetley bugs. You don't know what's good for you.'

'You're joking, Grandma.'

'I never joke,' she said. 'Beetles are perhaps best of all. They go *crunch*!'

'Grandma! That's beastly!'

The old hag grinned, showing those pale brown teeth. 'Sometimes, if you're lucky,' she said, 'you get a beetle inside the stem of a stick of celery. That's what I like.'

'Grandma! How *could* you?'

'You find all sorts of nice things in sticks of raw celery,' the old woman went on. 'Sometimes it's earwigs.'

'I don't want to hear about it!' cried George.

'A big fat earwig is very tasty,' Grandma said, licking her lips. 'But you've got to be very quick, my dear, when you put one of those in your mouth. It has a pair of sharp nippers on its back end and if it grabs your tongue with those, it never lets go. So you've got to bite the earwig first, *chop chop*, before it bites you.'

George started edging towards the door. He wanted to get as far away as possible from this filthy old woman.

'You're trying to get away from me, aren't you?' she said, pointing a finger straight at George's face. 'You're trying to get away from Grandma.'

Little George stood by the door staring at the old hag in the chair. She stared back at him.

Could it be, George wondered, that she was a witch? He had always thought witches were only in fairy tales, but now he was not so sure.

'Come closer to me, little boy,' she said, beckoning to him with a horny finger. 'Come closer to me and I will tell you *secrets*.'

George didn't move.

Grandma didn't move either.

'I know a great many secrets,' she said, and suddenly she smiled. It was a thin icy smile, the kind a snake might make just before it bites you. 'Come over here to Grandma and she'll whisper secrets to you.'

George took a step backwards, edging closer to the door.

'You mustn't be frightened of your old Grandma,' she said, smiling that icy smile.

George took another step backwards.

'Some of us,' she said, and all at once she was leaning forward in her chair and whispering in a throaty sort of voice George had never heard her use before. 'Some of us,' she said, 'have magic powers that can twist the creatures of this earth into wondrous shapes . . .'

A tingle of electricity flashed down the length of George's spine. He began to feel frightened.

'Some of us,' the old woman went on, 'have fire on our tongues and sparks in our bellies and wizardry in the tips of our fingers . . .

'Some of us know secrets that would make your hair stand straight up on end and your eyes pop out of their sockets . . .'

George wanted to run away, but his feet seemed stuck to the floor.

'We know how to make your nails drop off and teeth grow out of your fingers instead.'

George began to tremble. It was her face that frightened him most of all, the frosty smile, the brilliant unblinking eyes.

'We know how to have you wake up in the morning with a long tail coming out from behind you.'

'Grandma!' he cried out. 'Stop!'

'We know secrets, my dear, about dark places where dark things live and squirm and slither all over each other . . .'

George made a dive for the door.

'It doesn't matter how far you run,' he heard her saying, 'you won't ever get away . . .'

George ran into the kitchen, slamming the door behind him.

Chapter Two

THE MARVELLOUS PLAN

George sat himself down at the table in the kitchen. He was shaking a little. Oh, how he hated Grandma! He really *hated* that horrid old witchy woman. And all of a sudden he had a tremendous urge to *do something* about her. Something *whopping*. Something *absolutely terrific*. A *real shocker*. A sort of explosion. He wanted to blow away the witchy smell that hung about her in the next room. He may have been only eight years old but he was a brave little boy. He was ready to take this old woman on.

'I'm not going to be frightened by *her*,' he said softly to himself. But he *was* frightened. And that's why he wanted suddenly to explode her away.

Well . . . not quite away. But he did want to shake the old woman up a bit.

Very well, then. What should it be, this whopping terrific exploding shocker for Grandma?

He would have liked to put a firework banger under her chair but he didn't have one.

He would have liked to put a long green snake down the back of her dress but he didn't have a long green snake.

He would have liked to put six big black rats in the room with her and lock the door but he didn't have six big black rats.

As George sat there pondering this interesting problem, his eye fell upon the bottle of Grandma's brown medicine standing on the sideboard. Rotten stuff it seemed to be. Four times a day a large spoonful of it was shovelled into her mouth and it didn't do her the

slightest bit of good. She was always just as horrid after she'd had it as she'd been before. The whole point of medicine, surely, was to make a person better. If it didn't do that, then it was quite useless.

So-ho! thought George suddenly. *Ah-ha! Ho-hum!* I know exactly what I'll do. I shall make her a *new* medicine, one that is so strong and so fierce and so fantastic it will either cure her completely or blow off the top of her head. I'll make her a *magic medicine*, a medicine no doctor in the world has ever made before.

George looked at the kitchen clock. It said five past ten. There was nearly an hour left before Grandma's next dose was due at eleven.

'Here we go, then!' cried George, jumping up from the table. 'A magic medicine it shall be!'

'So give me a bug and a jumping flea,
Give me two snails and lizards three,
And a slimy squiggler from the sea,
And the poisonous sting of a bumblebee,
And the juice from the fruit of the ju-jube tree,
And the powdered bone of a wombat's knee.
And one hundred other things as well
Each with a rather nasty smell.
I'll stir them up, I'll boil them long,
A mixture tough, a mixture strong.
And then, heigh-ho, and down it goes,
A nice big spoonful (hold your nose)
Just gulp it down and have no fear.
"How do you like it, Granny dear?"
Will she go pop? Will she explode?
Will she go flying down the road?
Will she go poof in a puff of smoke?
Start fizzing like a can of Coke?
Who knows? Not I. Let's wait and see.
(I'm glad it's neither you nor me.)
Oh Grandma, if you only knew
What I have got in store for you!'

Chapter Three

GEORGE BEGINS TO MAKE THE MEDICINE

*G*eorge took an enormous saucepan out of the cupboard and placed it on the kitchen table.

'George!' came the shrill voice from the next room. 'What are you doing?'

'Nothing, Grandma,' he called out.

'You needn't think I can't hear you just because you closed the door! You're rattling the saucepans!'

'I'm just tidying the kitchen, Grandma.'

Then there was silence.

George had absolutely no doubts whatsoever about how he was going to make his famous medicine. He wasn't going to fool about wondering whether to put in a little bit of this or a little bit of that. Quite simply, he was going to put in EVERYTHING he could find. There would be no messing about, no hesitating, no wondering whether a particular thing would knock the old girl sideways or not. The rule would be this: whatever he saw, if it was runny or powdery or gooey, in it went.

Nobody had ever made a medicine like that before. If it didn't actually cure Grandma, then it would anyway cause some exciting results. It would be worth watching.

George decided to work his way round the various rooms one at a time and see what they had to offer.

He would go first to the bathroom. There are always lots of

funny things in a bathroom. So upstairs he went, carrying the enormous two-handled saucepan before him.

In the bathroom, he gazed longingly at the famous and dreaded medicine cupboard. But he didn't go near it. It was the only thing in the entire house he was forbidden to touch. He had made solemn promises to his parents about this and he wasn't going to break them. There were things in there, they had told him, that could actually kill a person, and although he was out to give Grandma a pretty fiery mouthful, he didn't really want a dead body on his hands. George put the saucepan on the floor and went to work.

15

Number one was a bottle labelled GOLDEN GLOSS HAIR SHAMPOO. He emptied it into the pan. 'That ought to wash her tummy nice and clean,' he said.

He took a full tube of TOOTHPASTE and squeezed out the whole lot of it in one long worm. 'Maybe that will brighten up those horrid brown teeth of hers,' he said.

16

There was an aerosol can of SUPERFOAM SHAVING SOAP belonging to his father. George loved playing with aerosols. He pressed the button and kept his finger on it until there was nothing left. A wonderful mountain of white foam built up in the giant saucepan.

With his fingers, he scooped out the contents of a jar of VITAMIN ENRICHED FACE CREAM.

In went a small bottle of scarlet NAIL VARNISH. 'If the toothpaste doesn't clean her teeth,' George said, 'then this will paint them as red as roses.'

He found another jar of creamy stuff labelled HAIR REMOVER. SMEAR IT ON YOUR LEGS, it said, AND ALLOW TO REMAIN FOR FIVE MINUTES. George tipped it all into the saucepan.

There was a bottle with yellow stuff inside it called DISHWORTH'S FAMOUS DANDRUFF CURE. In it went.

There was something called BRILLIDENT FOR CLEANING FALSE TEETH. It was a white powder. In that went, too.

He found another aerosol can, NEVERMORE PONKING DEODORANT SPRAY, GUARANTEED, it said, TO KEEP AWAY UNPLEASANT BODY SMELLS FOR A WHOLE DAY. 'She could use plenty of that,' George said as he sprayed the entire canful into the saucepan.

LIQUID PARAFFIN, the next one was called. It was a big bottle. He hadn't the faintest idea what it did to you, but he poured it in anyway.

That, he thought, looking around him, was about all from the bathroom.

On his mother's dressing-table in the bedroom, George found yet another lovely aerosol can. It was called HELGA'S HAIRSET. HOLD TWELVE INCHES AWAY FROM THE HAIR AND SPRAY LIGHTLY. He squirted the whole lot into the saucepan. He *did* enjoy squirting these aerosols.

There was a bottle of perfume called FLOWERS OF TURNIPS. It smelled of old cheese. In it went.

And in, too, went a large round box of POWDER. It was called PINK PLASTER. There was a powder-puff on top and he threw that in as well for luck.

He found a couple of LIPSTICKS. He pulled the greasy red things out of their little cases and added them to the mixture.

The bedroom had nothing more to offer, so George carried the enormous saucepan downstairs again and trotted into the laundry-room where the shelves were full of all kinds of household items.

The first one he took down was a large box of SUPERWHITE FOR AUTOMATIC WASHING-MACHINES. DIRT, it said, WILL DISAPPEAR LIKE MAGIC. George didn't know whether Grandma was automatic or not, but she was certainly a dirty old woman. 'So she'd better have it all,' he said, tipping in the whole boxful.

Then there was a big tin of WAXWELL FLOOR POLISH. IT REMOVES FILTH AND FOUL MESSES FROM YOUR FLOOR AND LEAVES EVERYTHING SHINY BRIGHT, it said. George scooped the orange-coloured waxy stuff out of the tin and plonked it into the pan.

19

There was a round cardboard carton labelled FLEA POWDER
FOR DOGS. KEEP WELL AWAY
FROM THE DOG'S FOOD,
it said, BECAUSE THIS
POWDER, IF EATEN, WILL
MAKE THE DOG EXPLODE.
'Good,' said George,
pouring it all into the saucepan.

He found a box of CANARY SEED on the shelf. 'Perhaps it'll
make the old bird sing,' he said, and
in it went.

Next, George explored
the box with shoe-
cleaning materials –
brushes and tins and
dusters. Well now,
he thought, Grandma's medicine is brown, so *my* medicine must
also be brown or she'll smell a rat. The way to colour it, he
decided, would be with BROWN SHOE-POLISH. The large tin he
chose was labelled DARK TAN. Splendid. He scooped it all out with
an old spoon and plopped it into the pan. He would stir it up later.

On his way back to the kitchen, George saw a bottle of GIN
standing on the sideboard. Grandma was very fond of gin.
She was allowed to have a small nip of it every evening. Now he
would give her a treat. He would pour in the whole bottle.
He did.

Back in the kitchen, George put the huge saucepan on the table
and went over to the cupboard that served as a larder. The
shelves were bulging with bottles and jars of every sort. He chose
the following and emptied them one by one into the saucepan:

A TIN OF CURRY POWDER

A TIN OF MUSTARD POWDER

A BOTTLE OF 'EXTRA HOT' CHILLI SAUCE

A TIN OF BLACK PEPPERCORNS

A BOTTLE OF HORSERADISH SAUCE

'There!' he said aloud. 'That should do it!'

'George!' came the screechy voice from the next room. 'Who are you talking to in there? What are you up to?'

'Nothing, Grandma, absolutely nothing,' he called back.

'Is it time for my medicine yet?'

'No, Grandma, not for about half an hour.'

'Well, just see you don't forget it.'

'I won't, Grandma,' George answered. 'I promise I won't.'

Chapter Four

ANIMAL PILLS

At this point, George suddenly had an extra good wheeze. Although the medicine cupboard in the house was forbidden ground, what about the medicines his father kept on the shelf in the shed next to the henhouse? The animal medicines?

What about *those*?

Nobody had ever told him he mustn't touch *them*.

Let's face it, George said to himself, hair-spray and shaving-cream and shoe-polish are all very well and they will no doubt cause some splendid explosions inside the old geezer, but what the magic mixture now needs is a touch of the real stuff, real pills and real tonics, to give it punch and muscle.

George picked up the heavy three-quarters full saucepan and carried it out of the back door. He crossed the farmyard and headed straight for the shed alongside the henhouse. He knew his father wouldn't be there. He was out haymaking in one of the meadows.

George entered the dusty old shed and put the saucepan on the bench. Then he looked up at the medicine shelf. There were five big bottles there. Two were full of pills, two were full of runny stuff and one was full of powder.

'I'll use them all,' George said. 'Grandma needs them. Boy, does she need them!'

The first bottle he took down contained an orange-coloured powder. The label said, FOR CHICKENS WITH FOUL PEST, HEN GRIPE, SORE BEAKS, GAMMY LEGS, COCKERELITIS, EGG TROUBLE, BROODINESS OR LOSS OF FEATHERS. MIX ONE SPOONFUL ONLY WITH EACH BUCKET OF FEED.

'Well,' George said aloud to himself as he tipped in the whole bottleful, 'the old bird won't be losing any feathers after she's had a dose of this.'

The next bottle he took down had about five hundred gigantic purple pills in it. FOR HORSES WITH HOARSE THROATS, it said

on the label. THE HOARSE-THROATED HORSE SHOULD SUCK ONE
PILL TWICE A DAY.

'Grandma may not have a hoarse throat,' George said, 'but
she's certainly got a sharp tongue. Maybe they'll cure that instead.'
Into the saucepan went the five hundred gigantic purple pills.

Then there was a bottle of thick yellowish liquid. FOR COWS,
BULLS AND BULLOCKS, the label said. WILL CURE COW POX, COW
MANGE, CRUMPLED HORNS, BAD BREATH IN BULLS, EARACHE,
TOOTHACHE, HEADACHE, HOOF-ACHE, TAILACHE AND SORE UDDERS.

'That grumpy old cow in the living-room has every one of those
rotten illnesses,' George said. 'She'll need it all.' With a slop and a
gurgle, the yellow liquid splashed into the now nearly full saucepan.

The next bottle contained a brilliant red liquid. SHEEPDIP, it said
on the label. FOR SHEEP WITH SHEEPROT AND FOR GETTING RID
OF TICKS AND FLEAS. MIX ONE SPOONFUL IN ONE GALLON OF
WATER AND SLOSH IT OVER THE SHEEP. CAUTION, DO NOT MAKE
THE MIXTURE ANY STRONGER OR THE WOOL WILL FALL OUT AND
THE ANIMAL WILL BE NAKED.

'By gum,' said George, 'how I'd love to walk in and slosh it all
over old Grandma and watch the ticks and fleas go jumping off her.
But I can't. I mustn't. So she'll have to drink it instead.' He poured
the bright red medicine into the saucepan.

The last bottle on the shelf was full of pale green pills. PIG PILLS,
the label announced. FOR PIGS WITH PORK PRICKLES, TENDER
TROTTERS, BRISTLE BLIGHT AND SWINE SICKNESS. GIVE ONE PILL
PER DAY. IN SEVERE CASES TWO PILLS MAY BE GIVEN, BUT MORE
THAN THAT WILL MAKE THE PIG ROCK AND ROLL.

'Just the stuff,' said George, 'for that miserable old pig back
there in the house. She'll need a very big dose.' He tipped all the
green pills, hundreds and hundreds of them, into the saucepan.

There was an old stick lying on the bench that had been used for stirring paint. George picked it up and started to stir his marvellous concoction. The mixture was as thick as cream, and as he stirred and stirred, many wonderful colours rose up from the depths and blended together, pinks, blues, greens, yellows and browns.

George went on stirring until it was all well mixed, but even so there were still hundreds of pills lying on the bottom that hadn't melted. And there was his mother's splendid powder-puff floating on the surface. 'I shall have to boil it all up,' George said. 'One good quick boil on the stove is all it

25

needs.' And with that he staggered back towards the house with the enormous heavy saucepan.

On the way, he passed the garage, so he went in to see if he could find any other interesting things. He added the following:

Half a pint of ENGINE OIL – to keep Grandma's engine going smoothly.

Some ANTI-FREEZE – to keep her radiator from freezing up in winter.

A handful of GREASE – to grease her creaking joints.

Then back to the kitchen.

Chapter Five

THE COOK-UP

In the kitchen, George put the saucepan on the stove and turned up the gas flame underneath it as high as it would go.

'George!' came the awful voice from the next room. 'It's time for my medicine!'

'Not yet, Grandma,' George called back. 'There's still twenty minutes before eleven o'clock.'

'What mischief are you up to in there now?' Granny screeched. 'I hear noises.'

George thought it best not to answer this one. He found a long wooden spoon in a kitchen drawer and began stirring hard. The stuff in the pot got hotter and hotter.

Soon the marvellous mixture began to froth and foam. A rich blue smoke, the colour of peacocks, rose from the surface of the liquid, and a fiery fearsome smell filled the kitchen. It made George choke and splutter. It was a smell unlike any he had smelled before. It was a brutal and bewitching smell, spicy and staggering, fierce and frenzied, full of wizardry and magic. Whenever he got a whiff of it up his nose, firecrackers went off in his skull and electric prickles ran along the backs of his legs.

It was wonderful to stand there stirring this amazing mixture and to watch it smoking blue and bubbling and frothing and foaming as though it were alive. At one point, he could have sworn he saw bright sparks flashing in the swirling foam. And suddenly, George found himself dancing around the steaming pot, chanting strange words that came into his head out of nowhere:

'Fiery broth and witch's brew
Foamy froth and riches blue
Fume and spume and spoondrift spray
Fizzle swizzle shout hooray
Watch it sloshing, swashing, sploshing
Hear it hissing, squishing, spissing
Grandma better start to pray.'

Chapter Six

BROWN PAINT

George turned off the heat under the saucepan. He must leave plenty of time for it to cool down.

When all the steam and froth had gone away, he peered into the giant pan to see what colour the great medicine now was. It was a deep and brilliant blue.

'It needs more brown in it,' George said. 'It simply must be brown or she'll get suspicious.'

George ran outside and dashed into his father's toolshed where all the paints were kept. There was a row of cans on the shelf, all colours, black, green, red, pink, white and brown. He reached for the can of brown. The label said simply DARK BROWN GLOSS PAINT ONE QUART. He took a screwdriver and prised off the lid. The can was three-quarters full. He rushed it back to the kitchen. He poured the whole lot into the saucepan. The saucepan was now full to the brim. Very gently, George stirred the paint into the mixture with the long wooden spoon. Ah-ha! It was all turning brown! A lovely rich creamy brown!

'Where's that medicine of mine, boy?!' came the voice from the living-room. 'You're forgetting me! You're doing it on purpose! I shall tell your mother!'

'I'm not forgetting you, Grandma,' George called back. 'I'm thinking of you all the time. But there are still ten minutes to go.'

'You're a nasty little maggot!' the voice screeched back. 'You're a lazy and disobedient little worm, and you're growing too fast.'

George fetched the bottle of Grandma's real medicine from the sideboard. He took out the cork and tipped it all down the sink. He then filled the bottle with his own magic mixture by dipping a small jug into the saucepan and using it as a pourer.

He replaced the cork.

Had it cooled down enough yet? Not quite. He held the bottle under the cold tap for a couple of minutes. The label came off in the wet but that didn't matter. He dried the bottle with a dishcloth.

All was now ready!

This was it!

The great moment had arrived!

'Medicine time, Grandma!' he called out.

'I should hope so, too,' came the grumpy reply.

The silver tablespoon in which the medicine was always given lay ready on the kitchen sideboard. George picked it up.

Holding the spoon in one hand and the bottle in the other, he advanced into the living-room.

Chapter Seven

GRANDMA GETS THE MEDICINE

Grandma sat hunched in her chair by the window. The wicked little eyes followed George closely as he crossed the room towards her.

'You're late,' she snapped.

'I don't think I am, Grandma.'

'Don't interrupt me in the middle of a sentence!' she shouted.

'But you'd finished your sentence, Grandma.'

'There you go again!' she cried. 'Always interrupting and arguing. You really are a tiresome little boy. What's the time?'

'It's exactly eleven o'clock, Grandma.'

'You're lying as usual. Stop talking so much and give me my medicine. Shake the bottle first. Then pour it into the spoon and make sure it's a whole spoonful.'

'Are you going to gulp it all down in one go?' George asked her. 'Or will you sip it?'

'What I do is none of your business,' the old woman said. 'Fill the spoon.'

As George removed the cork and began very slowly to pour the thick brown stuff into the spoon, he couldn't help thinking back upon all the mad and marvellous things that had gone into the making of this crazy stuff – the shaving soap, the hair remover, the dandruff cure, the automatic washing-machine powder, the flea powder for dogs, the shoe-polish, the black pepper, the horseradish sauce and all the rest of them, not to mention the powerful animal pills and powders and liquids . . . and the brown paint.

'Open your mouth wide, Grandma,' he said, 'and I'll pop it in.'

The old hag opened her small wrinkled mouth, showing disgusting pale brown teeth.

'Here we go!' George cried out. 'Swallow it down!' He pushed the spoon well into her mouth and tipped the mixture down her throat. Then he stepped back to watch the result.

It was worth watching.

Grandma yelled '*Oweeeee!*' and her whole body shot up *whoosh* into the air. It was exactly as though someone had pushed an electric wire through the underneath of her chair and switched on the current. Up she went like a jack-in-the-box . . . and she didn't come down . . . she stayed there . . . suspended in mid-air . . . about two feet up . . . still in a sitting position . . . but rigid now . . . frozen . . . quivering . . . the eyes bulging . . . the hair standing straight up on end.

'Is something wrong, Grandma?' George asked her politely. 'Are you all right?'

Suspended up there in space, the old girl was beyond speaking.

The shock that George's marvellous mixture had given her must have been tremendous.

You'd have thought she'd swallowed a red-hot poker the way she took off from that chair.

Then down she came again with a *plop*, back into her seat.

'Call the fire brigade!' she shouted suddenly. 'My stomach's on fire!'

'It's just the medicine, Grandma,' George said. 'It's good strong stuff.'

'Fire!' the old woman yelled. 'Fire in the basement! Get a bucket! Man the hoses! Do something quick!'

'Cool it, Grandma,' George said. But he got a bit of a shock when he saw the smoke coming out of her mouth and out of her nostrils. Clouds of black smoke were coming out of her nose and blowing around the room.

'By golly, you really are on fire,' George said.

'Of course I'm on fire!' she yelled. 'I'll be burned to a crisp! I'll be fried to a frizzle! I'll be boiled like a beetroot!'

George ran into the kitchen and came back with a jug of water. 'Open your mouth, Grandma!' he cried. He could hardly see her for the smoke, but he managed to pour half a jugful down her throat. A sizzling sound, the kind you get if you hold a hot frying-pan under a cold tap, came up from deep down in Grandma's stomach. The old hag bucked and shied and snorted. She gasped and gurgled. Spouts of water came shooting out of her. And the smoke cleared away.

'The fire's out,' George announced proudly. 'You'll be all right now, Grandma.'

'*All right?*' she yelled. 'Who's *all right?* There's jacky-jumpers in my tummy! There's squigglers in my belly! There's bangers in my bottom!' She began bouncing up and down in the chair. Quite obviously she was not very comfortable.

'You'll find it's doing you a lot of good, that medicine, Grandma,' George said.

'*Good?*' she screamed. 'Doing me *good?* It's *killing* me!'

Then she began to bulge.

She was swelling!

She was puffing up all over!

Someone was pumping her up, that's how it looked!

Was she going to explode?

Her face was turning from purple to green!

GEORGE'S MARVELLOUS MEDICINE

But wait! She had a puncture somewhere! George could hear the hiss of escaping air. She stopped swelling. She was going down. She was slowly getting thinner again, shrinking back and back slowly to her shrively old self.

'How's things, Grandma?' George said.

No answer.

Then a funny thing happened. Grandma's body gave a sudden sharp twist and a sudden sharp jerk and she flipped herself clear out of the chair and landed neatly on her two feet on the carpet.

'That's terrific, Grandma!' George cried. 'You haven't stood up like that for years! Look at you! You're standing up all on your own and you're not even using a stick!'

Grandma didn't even hear him. The frozen pop-eyed look was back with her again now. She was miles away in another world.

Marvellous medicine, George told himself. He found it fascinating to stand there watching what it was doing to the old hag. What next? he wondered.

He soon found out.

Suddenly she began to grow.

It was quite slow at first . . . just a very gradual inching upwards . . . up, up, up . . . inch by inch . . . getting taller and taller . . . about an inch every few seconds . . . and in the beginning George didn't notice it.

But when she had passed the five foot six mark and was going on up towards being six feet tall, George gave a jump and shouted, 'Hey, Grandma! You're *growing*! You're *going up*! Hang on, Grandma! You'd better stop now or you'll be hitting the ceiling!'

But Grandma didn't stop.

It was a truly fantastic sight, this ancient scrawny old woman getting taller and taller, longer and longer, thinner and thinner,

as though she were a piece of elastic being pulled upwards by invisible hands.

When the top of her head actually touched the ceiling, George thought she was bound to stop.

But she didn't.

There was a sort of scrunching noise, and bits of plaster and cement came raining down.

'Hadn't you better stop now, Grandma?' George said. 'Daddy's just had this whole room repainted.'

But there was no stopping her now.

Soon, her head and shoulders had completely disappeared through the ceiling and she was still going.

George dashed upstairs to his own bedroom and there she was coming up through the floor like a mushroom.

'Whoopee!' she shouted, finding her voice at last. 'Hallelujah, here I come!'

'Steady on, Grandma,' George said.

'With a heigh-nonny-no and up we go!' she shouted. 'Just watch me grow!'

'This is *my* room,' George said. 'Look at the mess you're making.'

'Terrific medicine!' she cried. 'Give me some more!'

She's dotty as a doughnut, George thought.

'Come on, boy! Give me some more!' she yelled. 'Dish it out! I'm slowing down!'

George was still clutching the medicine bottle in one hand and the spoon in the other. Oh well, he thought, why not? He poured out a second dose and popped it into her mouth.

'*Oweee!*' she screamed and up she went again. Her feet were still on the floor downstairs in the living-room but her head was

moving quickly towards the ceiling of the bedroom.

'I'm on my way now, boy!' she called down to George.
'Just watch me go!'

'That's the attic above you, Grandma!' George called out.
'I'd keep out of there! It's full of bugs and bogles!'

Crash! The old girl's head went through the ceiling as though it
were butter.

George stood in his bedroom gazing at the shambles. There was
a big hole in the floor and another in the ceiling, and sticking up
like a post between the two was the middle part of Grandma.
Her legs were in the room below, her head in the attic.

'I'm still going!' came the old screechy voice from up above. 'Give me another dose, my boy, and let's go through the roof!'

'No, Grandma, no!' George called back. 'You're busting up the whole house!'

'To heck with the house!' she shouted. 'I want some fresh air! I haven't been outside for twenty years!'

'By golly, she *is* going through the roof!' George told himself. He ran downstairs. He rushed out of the back door into the yard. It would be simply awful, he thought, if she bashed up the roof as well. His father would be furious. And he, George, would get the blame. *He* had made the medicine. *He* had given her too much. 'Don't come through the roof, Grandma,' he prayed. 'Please don't.'

Chapter Eight

THE BROWN HEN

*G*eorge stood in the farmyard looking up at the roof. The old farmhouse had a fine roof of pale red tiles and tall chimneys.

There was no sign of Grandma. There was only a song-thrush sitting on one of the chimney-pots, singing a song. The old wurzel's got stuck in the attic, George thought. Thank goodness for that.

Suddenly a tile came clattering down from the roof and fell into the yard. The song-thrush took off fast and flew away.

Then another tile came down.

Then half a dozen more.

And then, very slowly, like some weird monster rising up from the deep, Grandma's head came through the roof . . .

Then her scrawny neck . . .

And the tops of her shoulders . . .

'How'm I doing, boy!' she shouted. 'How's that for a bash up?'

'Don't you think you'd better stop now, Grandma?' George called out . . .

'I have stopped!' she answered. 'I feel terrific! Didn't I tell you I had magic powers! Didn't I warn you I had wizardry in the tips of my fingers! But you wouldn't listen to me, would you? You wouldn't listen to your old Grandma!'

'*You* didn't do it, Grandma,' George shouted back to her. '*I* did it! I made you a new medicine!'

'*A new medicine? You?* What rubbish!' she yelled.

'I did! I did!' George shouted.

'You're lying as usual!' Grandma yelled. 'You're always lying!'

'I'm not lying, Grandma. I swear I'm not.'

The wrinkled old face high up on the roof stared down suspiciously at George. 'Are you telling me you actually made a new medicine all by yourself?' she shouted.

'Yes, Grandma, all by myself.'

'I don't believe you,' she answered. 'But I'm very comfortable up here. Fetch me a cup of tea.'

A brown hen was pecking about in the yard close to where George was standing. The hen gave him an idea. Quickly, he uncorked the medicine bottle and poured some of the brown stuff into the spoon. 'Watch this, Grandma!' he shouted. He crouched down, holding out the spoon to the hen.

'Chicken,' he said. 'Chick-chick-chicken. Come here. Have some of this.'

Chickens are stupid birds, and very greedy. They think everything is food. This one thought the spoon was full of corn. It hopped over. It put its head on one side and looked at the spoon. 'Come on, chicken,' George said. 'Good chicken. Chick-chick-chick.'

The brown hen stretched out its neck towards the spoon and went *peck*. It got a beakful of medicine.

The effect was electric.

'*Oweee!*' shrieked the hen and it shot straight up into the air like a rocket. It went as high as the house.

Then down it came again into the yard, *splosh*. And there it sat with its feathers all sticking straight out from its body. There was a look of amazement on its silly face. George stood watching it. Grandma up on the roof was watching it, too.

The hen got to its feet. It was rather shaky. It was making funny gurgling noises in its throat. Its beak was opening and shutting. It seemed like a pretty sick hen.

'You've done it in, you stupid boy!' Grandma shouted. 'That hen's going to die! Your father'll be after you now! He'll give you socks and serve you right!'

All of a sudden, black smoke started pouring out of the hen's beak.

'It's on fire!' Grandma yelled. 'The hen's on fire!'

George ran to the water-trough to get a bucket of water.

'That hen'll be roasted and ready for eating any moment!' Grandma shouted.

George sloshed the bucket of water over the hen. There was a sizzling sound and the smoke went away.

'Old hen's laid its last egg!' Grandma shouted. 'Hens don't do any laying after they've been on fire!'

Now that the fire was out, the hen seemed better. It stood up properly. It flapped its wings. Then it crouched down low to the ground, as though getting ready to jump. It did jump. It jumped high in the air and turned a complete somersault, then landed back on its feet.

'It's a circus hen!' Grandma shouted from the rooftop. 'It's a flipping acrobat!'

Now the hen

began to

grow.

George had been waiting for this to happen. 'It's growing!' he yelled. 'It's growing, Grandma! Look, it's growing!'

Bigger and bigger . . . taller and taller it grew. Soon the hen was four or five times its normal size.

'Can you see it, Grandma?!' George shouted.

'I can see it, boy!' the old girl shouted back. 'I'm watching it!'

George was hopping about from one foot to the other with excitement, pointing at the enormous hen and shouting, 'It's had the magic medicine, Grandma, and it's growing just like you did!'

But there was a difference between the way the hen was growing and the way Grandma grew. When Grandma grew taller and taller, she got thinner and thinner. The hen didn't. It stayed nice and plump all along.

Soon it was taller than George, but it didn't stop there. It went right on growing until it was about as big as a horse. Then it stopped.

'Doesn't it look marvellous, Grandma!' George shouted.

'It's not as tall as me!' Grandma sang out. 'Compared with me, that hen is titchy small! I am the tallest of them all!'

Chapter Nine

THE PIG, THE BULLOCKS, THE SHEEP, THE PONY AND THE NANNY-GOAT

At that moment, George's mother came back from shopping in the village. She drove her car into the yard and got out. She was carrying a bottle of milk in one hand and a bag of groceries in the other.

The first thing she saw was the gigantic brown hen towering over little George. She dropped the bottle of milk.

Then Grandma started shouting at her from the rooftop, and when she looked up and saw Grandma's head sticking up through

the tiles, she dropped the bag of groceries.

'How about that then, eh, Mary?' Grandma shouted. 'I'll bet you've never seen a hen as big as that! That's George's giant hen, that is!'

'But . . . but . . . but . . .' stammered George's mother.

'It's George's magic medicine!' Grandma shouted. 'We've both of us had it, the hen and I!'

'But how in the world did you get up on the roof?' cried the mother.

'I didn't!' cackled the old woman. 'My feet are still standing on the floor in the living-room!'

This was too much for George's mother to understand. She just goggled and gaped. She looked as though she was going to faint.

A second later, George's father appeared. His name was Mr Killy Kranky. Mr Kranky was a small man with bandy legs and a huge head. He was a kind father to George, but he was not an easy person to live with because even the smallest things got him all worked up and excited. The hen standing in the yard was certainly not a small thing, and when Mr Kranky saw it he started jumping about as though something was burning his feet. 'Great heavens!' he cried, waving his arms. 'What's this? What's happened? Where did it come from? It's a giant hen! Who did it?'

'I did,' George said.

'Look at *me*!' Grandma shouted from the rooftop. 'Never mind about the hen! What about *me*?'

Mr Kranky looked up and saw Grandma. 'Shut up, Grandma,' he said. It didn't seem to surprise him that the old girl was sticking up through the roof. It was the hen that excited him. He had never seen anything like it. But then who had?

48

'It's fantastic!' Mr Kranky shouted, dancing round and round. 'It's colossal! It's gigantic! It's tremendous! It's a miracle! How did you do it, George?'

George started telling his father about the magic medicine. While he was doing this, the big brown hen sat down in the middle of the yard and went *cluck-cluck-cluck* . . . *cluck-cluck-cluck-cluck-cluck.*

Everyone stared at it.

When it stood up again, there was a brown egg lying there. The egg was the size of a football.

'That egg would make scrambled eggs for twenty people!' Mrs Kranky said.

'George!' Mr Kranky shouted. 'How much of this medicine have you got?'

'Lots,' George said. 'There's a big saucepanful in the kitchen, and this bottle here's nearly full.'

'Come with me!' Mr Kranky yelled, grabbing George by the arm. 'Bring the medicine! For years and years I've been trying to breed bigger and bigger animals. Bigger bulls for beef. Bigger pigs for pork. Bigger sheep for mutton . . .'

They went to the pigsty first.

George gave a spoonful of medicine to the pig.

The pig blew smoke from its nose and jumped about all over the place. Then it grew and grew.

In the end, it looked like this . . .

They went to the herd of fine black bullocks that Mr Kranky was trying to fatten for the market.

George gave each of them some medicine, and this is what happened . . .

Then the sheep . . .

He gave some to his grey pony, Jack Frost . . .

And finally,

just for fun,

he gave some
to Alma,

the nanny-goat . . .

Chapter Ten

A CRANE FOR GRANDMA

Grandma, from high up on the rooftop, could see everything that was going on and she didn't like what she saw. She wanted to be the centre of attention and nobody was taking the slightest notice of her. George and Mr Kranky were running round and getting excited about the enormous animals. Mrs Kranky was washing up in the kitchen, and Grandma was all alone on the rooftop.

'Hey you!' she yelled. 'George! Get me a cup of tea this minute, you idle little beast!'

'Don't listen to the old goat,' Mr Kranky said. 'She's stuck where she is and a good thing, too.'

'But we can't leave her up there, Dad,' George said. 'What if it rains?'

'George!' Grandma yelled. 'Oh, you horrible little boy! You disgusting little worm! Fetch me a cup of tea at once and a slice of currant cake!'

'We'll have to get her out, Dad,' George said. 'She won't give us any peace if we don't.'

Mrs Kranky came outside and she agreed with George. 'She's my own mother,' she said.

'She's a pain in the neck,' Mr Kranky said.

'I don't care,' Mrs Kranky said. 'I'm not leaving my own mother sticking up through the roof for the rest of her life.'

So in the end, Mr Kranky telephoned the Crane Company and asked them to send their biggest crane out to the house at once.

The crane arrived one hour later. It was on wheels and there were two men inside it. The crane men climbed up on to the roof and put ropes under Grandma's arms. Then she was lifted right up through the roof . . .

In a way, the medicine had done Grandma good. It had not made her any less grumpy or bad-tempered, but it seemed to have cured all her aches and pains, and she was suddenly as frisky as a ferret. As soon as the crane had lowered her to the ground, she ran over to George's huge pony, Jack Frost, and jumped on to his back. This ancient old hag, who was now as tall as a house, then galloped about the farm on the gigantic pony, jumping over trees and sheds and shouting,

'Out of my way! Clear the decks! Stand back, all you miserable midgets or I'll trample you to death!' and other silly things like that.

But because Grandma was now much too tall to get back into the house, she had to sleep that night in the hay-barn with the mice and the rats.

Chapter Eleven

MR KRANKY'S GREAT IDEA

The next day, George's father came down to breakfast in a state of greater excitement than ever. 'I've been awake all night thinking about it!' he cried.

'About what, Dad?' George asked him.

'About your marvellous medicine, of course! We can't stop now, my boy! We must start making more of it at once! More and more and more!'

The giant saucepan had been completely emptied the day before because there had been so many sheep and pigs and cows and bullocks to be dosed.

'But why do we need more, Dad?' George asked. 'We've done all our own animals and we've made Grandma feel as frisky as a ferret even though she does have to sleep in the barn.'

'My dear boy,' cried Mr Killy Kranky, 'we need barrels and barrels of it! Tons and tons! Then we will sell it to every farmer in the world so that all of them can have giant animals! We will build a Marvellous Medicine Factory and sell the stuff in bottles at five pounds a time. We will become rich and you will become famous!'

'But wait a minute, Dad,' George said.

'There's no waiting!' cried Mr Kranky, working himself up so much that he put butter in his coffee and milk on his toast. 'Don't you understand what this tremendous invention of yours is going to do to the world! Nobody will ever go hungry again!'

'Why won't they?' asked George.

'Because one giant cow will give fifty buckets of milk a day!' cried Mr Kranky, waving his arms. 'One giant chicken will make a hundred fried chicken dinners, and one giant pig will give you a thousand pork chops! It's tremendous, my dear boy! It's fantastic! It'll change the world.'

'But wait a minute, Dad,' George said again.

'Don't keep saying wait a minute!' shouted Mr Kranky. 'There isn't a minute to *wait*! We must get cracking at once!'

'Do calm down, my dear,' Mrs Kranky said from the other end of the table. 'And stop putting marmalade on your cornflakes.'

'The heck with my cornflakes!' cried Mr Kranky, leaping up from his chair. 'Come on, George! Let's get going! And the first thing we'll do is to make one more saucepanful as a tester.'

'But Dad,' said little George. 'The trouble is . . .'

'There won't be any trouble, my boy!' cried Mr Kranky. 'How can there possibly be any trouble? All you've got to do is put the same stuff into the saucepan as you did yesterday. And while you're doing it, I'll write down each and every item. That's how we'll get the magic recipe!'

'But Dad,' George said. 'Please listen to me.'

'Why don't you listen to him?' Mrs Kranky said. 'The boy's trying to tell you something.'

But Mr Kranky was too excited to listen to anyone except himself. 'And then,' he cried, 'when the new mixture is ready, we'll test it out on an old hen just to make absolutely sure we've got it right, and after that we'll all shout hooray and build the giant factory!'

'But Dad . . .'

'Come on then, what is it you want to say?'

'I can't possibly remember all the hundreds of things I put into the saucepan to make the medicine,' George said.

'Of course you can, my dear boy,' cried Mr Kranky. 'I'll help you! I'll jog your memory! You'll get it in the end, you see if you don't! Now then, what was the very first thing you put in?'

'I went up to the bathroom first,' George said. 'I used a lot of things in the bathroom and on Mummy's dressing-table.'

'Come on, then!' cried Mr Killy Kranky. 'Up we go to the bathroom!'

When they got there, they found, of course, a whole lot of empty tubes and empty aerosols and empty bottles. 'That's great,' said Mr Kranky. 'That tells us exactly what you used. If anything is empty, it means you used it.'

So Mr Kranky started making a list of everything that was empty in the bathroom. Then they went to Mrs Kranky's dressing-table. 'A box of powder,' said Mr Kranky, writing it down. 'Helga's hairset. Flowers of Turnips perfume. Terrific. This is going to be easy. Where did you go next?'

'To the laundry-room,' George said. 'But are you sure you haven't missed anything out up here, Dad?'

'That's up to you, my boy,' Mr Kranky said. 'Have I?'

'I don't think so,' George said. So down they went to the laundry-room and once again Mr Kranky wrote down the names of all the empty bottles and cans. 'My goodness me, what a mass of stuff you used!' he cried. 'No wonder it did magic things! Is that the lot?'

'No, Dad, it's not,' George said, and he led his father out to the shed where the animal medicines were kept and showed him the five big empty bottles up on the shelf. Mr Kranky wrote down all their names.

'Anything else?' Mr Kranky asked.

Little George scratched his head and thought and thought but he couldn't remember having put anything else in.

Mr Killy Kranky leapt into his car and drove down to the village and bought new bottles and tubes and cans of everything on his list. He then went to the vet and got a fresh supply of all the animal medicines George had used.

'Now show me how you did it, George,' he said. 'Come along. Show me exactly how you mixed them all together.'

Chapter Twelve

MARVELLOUS MEDICINE NUMBER TWO

They were in the kitchen now and the big saucepan was on the stove. All the things Mr Kranky had bought were lined up near the sink.

'Come along, my boy!' cried Mr Killy Kranky. 'Which one did you put in first?'

'This one,' George said. 'Golden Gloss Hair Shampoo.' He emptied the bottle into the pan.

'Now the toothpaste,' George went on . . . 'And the shaving soap . . . and the face cream . . . and the nail varnish . . .'

'Keep at it, my boy!' cried Mr Kranky, dancing round the kitchen. 'Keep putting them in! Don't stop! Don't pause! Don't hesitate! It's a pleasure, my dear fellow, to watch you work!'

One by one, George poured and squeezed the things into the saucepan. With everything so close at hand, the whole job didn't take him more than ten minutes. But when it was all done, the saucepan didn't somehow seem to be quite as full as it had been the first time.

'*Now* what did you do?' cried Mr Kranky. 'Did you stir it?'

'I boiled it,' George said. 'But not for long. And I stirred it as well.'

So Mr Kranky lit the gas under the saucepan and George stirred the mixture with the same long wooden spoon he had used before. 'It's not brown enough,' George said. 'Wait a minute! I know what I've forgotten!'

'What?' cried Mr Kranky. 'Tell me, quick! Because if we've forgotten even one tiny thing, then it won't work! At least not in the same way.'

'A quart of brown gloss paint,' George said. 'That's what I've forgotten.'

Mr Killy Kranky shot out of the house and into his car like a rocket. He sped down to the village and bought the paint and rushed back again. He opened the can in the kitchen and handed it to George. George poured the paint into the saucepan.

'Ah-ha, that's better,' George said. 'That's more like the right colour.'

'It's boiling!' cried Mr Kranky. 'It's boiling and bubbling, George! Is it ready yet?'

'It's ready,' George said. 'At least I hope it is.'

'Right!' shouted Mr Kranky, hopping about. 'Let's test it! Let's give some to a chicken!'

'My heavens alive, why don't you calm down a bit?' Mrs Kranky said, coming into the kitchen.

'*Calm down?*' cried Mr Kranky. 'You expect me to *calm down* and here we are mixing up the greatest medicine ever discovered in the history of the world! Come along, George! Dip a cupful out of the saucepan and get a spoon and we'll give some to a chicken just to make absolutely certain we've got the correct mixture.'

Outside in the yard, there were several chickens that hadn't had any of George's Marvellous Medicine Number One. They were pecking about in the dirt in that silly way chickens do.

George crouched down, holding out a spoonful of Marvellous Medicine Number Two. 'Come on, chicken,' he said. 'Good chicken. Chick-chick-chick.'

A white chicken with black specks on its feathers looked up at George. It walked over to the spoon and went *peck*.

The effect that Medicine Number Two had on this chicken was not quite the same as the effect produced by Medicine Number One, but it was very interesting. '*Whooosh!*' shrieked the chicken and it shot six feet up in the air and came down again. Then *sparks* came flying out of its beak, bright yellow sparks of fire, as though someone was sharpening a knife on a grindstone inside its tummy. Then its legs began to grow longer. Its body stayed the same size but the two thin yellow legs got longer and longer and longer . . . and longer still . . .

'What's happening to it?' cried Mr Killy Kranky.

'Something's wrong,' George said.

The legs went on growing and the more they grew, the higher up into the air went the chicken's body. When the legs were about fifteen feet long, they stopped growing. The chicken looked perfectly absurd with its long long legs and its ordinary little body perched high up on top. It was like a chicken on stilts.

'Oh my sainted aunts!' cried Mr Killy Kranky. 'We've got it wrong! This chicken's no good to anybody! It's all legs! No one wants chickens' legs!'

'I must have left something out,' George said.

'I *know* you left something out!' cried Mr Kranky. 'Think, boy, think! What was it you left out?'

'I've got it!' said George.

'What was it, quick?'

'Flea powder for dogs,' George said.

'You mean you put *flea* powder in the first one?'

'Yes, Dad, I did. A whole carton of it.'

'Then that's the answer!'

'Wait a minute,' said George. 'Did we have brown shoe-polish on our list?'

'We did not,' said Mr Kranky.

'I used that, too,' said George.

'Well, no *wonder* it went wrong,' said Mr Kranky. He was already running to his car, and soon he was heading down to the village to buy more flea powder and more shoe-polish.

Chapter Thirteen

MARVELLOUS MEDICINE NUMBER THREE

'Here it is!' cried Mr Killy Kranky, rushing into the kitchen. 'One carton of flea powder for dogs and one tin of brown shoe-polish!'

George poured the flea powder into the giant saucepan. Then he scooped the shoe-polish out of its tin and added that as well.

'Stir it up, George!' shouted Mr Kranky. 'Give it another boil! We've got it this time! I'll bet we've got it!'

After Marvellous Medicine Number Three had been boiled and stirred, George took a cupful of it out into the yard to try it on another chicken. Mr Kranky ran after him, flapping his arms and hopping with excitement. 'Come and watch this one!' he called out to Mrs Kranky. 'Come and watch us turning an ordinary chicken into a lovely great big one that lays eggs as large as footballs!'

'I hope you do better than last time,' said Mrs Kranky, following them out.

'Come on, chicken,' said George, holding out a spoonful of Medicine Number Three. 'Good chicken. Chick-chick-chick-chick-chick. Have some of this lovely medicine.'

A magnificent black cockerel with a scarlet comb came stepping over. The cockerel looked at the spoon and it went *peck*.

'*Cock-a-doodle-do!*' squawked the cockerel, shooting up into the air and coming down again.

'Watch him now!' cried Mr Kranky. 'Watch him grow! Any moment he's going to start getting bigger and bigger!'

Mr Killy Kranky, Mrs Kranky and little George stood in the yard staring at the black cockerel. The cockerel stood quite still. It looked as though it had a headache.

'What's happening to its neck?' Mrs Kranky said.

'It's getting longer,' George said.

'I'll say it's getting longer,' Mrs Kranky said.

Mr Kranky, for once, said nothing.

'Last time it was the legs,' Mrs Kranky said. 'Now it's the neck. Who wants a chicken with a long neck? You can't eat a chicken's neck.'

It was an extraordinary sight. The cockerel's body hadn't grown at all. But the neck was now about six feet long.

'All right, George,' Mr Kranky said. 'What else have you forgotten?'

'I don't know,' George said.

'Oh yes you do,' Mr Kranky said. 'Come along, boy, *think*. There's probably just one vital thing missing and you've got to remember it.'

'I put in some engine oil from the garage,' George said. 'Did you have that on your list?'

'Eureka!' cried Mr Kranky. 'That's the answer! How much did you put in?'

'Half a pint,' George said.

Mr Kranky ran to the garage and found another half-pint of oil. 'And some anti-freeze,' George called after him. 'I sloshed in a bit of anti-freeze.'

Chapter Fourteen

MARVELLOUS MEDICINE
NUMBER FOUR

Back in the kitchen once again, George, with Mr Kranky watching him anxiously, tipped half a pint of engine oil and some anti-freeze into the giant saucepan.

'Boil it up again!' cried Mr Kranky. 'Boil it and stir it!'

George boiled it and stirred it.

'You'll never get it right,' said Mrs Kranky. 'Don't forget you don't just have to have the same things but you've got to have exactly the same *amounts* of those things. And how can you possibly do that?'

'You keep out of this!' cried Mr Kranky. 'We're doing fine! We've got it this time, you see if we haven't!'

This was George's Marvellous Medicine Number Four, and when it had boiled for a couple of minutes, George once again carried a cupful of it out into the yard. Mr Kranky ran after him. Mrs Kranky followed more slowly. 'You're going to have some mighty queer chickens around here if you go on like this,' she said.

'Dish it out, George!' cried Mr Kranky. 'Give a spoonful to that one over there!' He pointed to a brown hen.

George knelt down and held out the spoon with the new medicine in it. 'Chick-chick,' he said. 'Try some of this.'

The brown hen walked over and looked at the spoon. Then it went *peck*.

'*Owch!*' it said. Then a funny whistling noise came out of its beak.

'Watch it grow!' shouted Mr Kranky.

'Don't be too sure,' said Mrs Kranky. 'Why is it whistling like that?'

'Keep quiet, woman!' cried Mr Kranky. 'Give it a chance!'

They stood there staring at the brown hen. ·

'It's getting smaller,' George said. 'Look at it, Dad. It's shrinking.'

And indeed it was. In less than a minute, the hen had shrunk so much it was no bigger than a new-hatched chick. It looked ridiculous.

Chapter Fifteen

GOODBYE GRANDMA

'There's still something you've left out,' Mr Kranky said.

'I can't think what it could be,' George said.

'Give it up,' Mrs Kranky said. 'Pack it in. You'll never get it right.'

Mr Kranky looked very forlorn.

George looked pretty fed up, too. He was still kneeling on the ground with the spoon in one hand and the cup full of medicine in the other. The ridiculous tiny brown hen was walking slowly away.

At that point, Grandma came striding into the yard. From her enormous height, she glared down at the three people below her and she shouted, 'What's going on around here? Why hasn't anyone brought me my morning cup of tea? It's bad enough having to sleep in the yard with the rats and mice but I'll be blowed if I'm going to starve as well! No tea! No eggs and bacon! No buttered toast!'

'I'm sorry, Mother,' Mrs Kranky said. 'We've been terribly busy. I'll get you something right away.'

'Let George get it, the lazy little brute!' Grandma shouted.

Just then, the old woman spotted the cup in George's hand. She bent down and peered into it. She saw that it was full of brown liquid. It looked very much like tea. 'Ho-ho!' she cried. 'Ha-ha! So that's your little game, is it! You look after yourself all right, don't you! You make quite sure *you've* got a nice cup of morning tea! But you didn't think to bring one to your poor old Grandma! I always knew you were a selfish pig!'

'No, Grandma,' George said. 'This isn't . . .'

'Don't lie to me, boy!' the enormous old hag shouted. 'Pass it up here this minute!'

'No!' cried Mrs Kranky. 'No, Mother, don't! That's not for you!'

'Now *you're* against me, too!' shouted Grandma. 'My own daughter trying to stop me having my breakfast! Trying to starve me out!'

Mr Kranky looked up at the horrid old woman and he smiled sweetly. 'Of course it's for you, Grandma,' he said. 'You take it and drink it while it's nice and hot.'

'Don't think I won't,' Grandma said, bending down from her great height and reaching out a huge horny hand for the cup. 'Hand it over, George.'

'No, no, Grandma!' George cried out, pulling the cup away. 'You mustn't! You're not to have it!'

'Give it to me, boy!' yelled Grandma.

'Don't!' cried Mrs Kranky. 'That's George's Marvellous . . .'

'Everything's George's round here!' shouted Grandma. 'George's this, George's that! I'm fed up with it!' She snatched the cup out of little George's hand and carried it high up out of reach.

'Drink it up, Grandma,' Mr Kranky said, grinning hugely. 'Lovely tea.'

'No!' the other two cried. 'No, no, no!'

But it was too late. The ancient beanpole had already put the cup to her lips, and in one gulp she swallowed everything that was in it.

'Mother!' wailed Mrs Kranky. 'You've just drunk fifty doses of George's Marvellous Medicine Number Four and look what one tiny spoonful did to that little old brown hen!'

But Grandma didn't even hear her. Great clouds of steam were already pouring out of her mouth and she was beginning to whistle.

'This is going to be interesting,' Mr Kranky said, still grinning.

'Now you've done it!' cried Mrs Kranky, glaring at her husband. 'You've cooked the old girl's goose!'

'I didn't do anything,' Mr Kranky said.

'Oh, yes you did! You told her to drink it!'

A tremendous hissing sound was coming from above their heads. Steam was shooting out of Grandma's mouth and nose and ears and whistling as it came.

'She'll feel better after she's let off a bit of steam,' Mr Kranky said.

'She's going to blow up!' Mrs Kranky wailed. 'Her boiler's going to burst!'

'Stand clear,' Mr Kranky said.

George was quite alarmed. He stood up and ran back a few paces. The jets of white steam kept squirting out of the skinny old hag's head, and the whistling was so high and shrill it hurt the ears.

'Call the fire brigade!' cried Mrs Kranky. 'Call the police! Man the hose-pipes!'

'Too late,' said Mr Kranky, looking pleased.

'Grandma!' shrieked Mrs Kranky. 'Mother! Run to the drinking-trough and put your head under the water!'

But even as she spoke, the whistling suddenly stopped and the steam disappeared. That was when Grandma began to get smaller. She had started off with her head as high as the roof of the house, but now she was coming down fast.

'Watch this, George!' Mr Kranky shouted, hopping around the yard and flapping his arms. 'Watch what happens when someone's had fifty spoonfuls instead of one!'

Very soon, Grandma was back to normal height.

'Stop!' cried Mrs Kranky. 'That's just right.'

But she didn't stop. Smaller and smaller she got . . . down and down she went. In another half minute she was no bigger than a bottle of lemonade.

'How d'you feel, Mother?' asked Mrs Kranky anxiously.

Grandma's tiny face still bore the same foul and furious expression it had always had. Her eyes, no bigger now than little keyholes, were blazing with anger. 'How do I *feel*?' she yelled. 'How d'you *think* I feel? How would *you* feel if you'd been a glorious giant a minute ago and suddenly you're a miserable midget?'

'She's still going!' shouted Mr Kranky gleefully. 'She's still getting smaller!'

And by golly, she was.

When she was no bigger than a cigarette, Mrs Kranky made a grab for her. She held her in her hands and she cried, 'How do I stop her getting smaller still?'

'You can't,' said Mr Kranky. 'She's had fifty times the right amount.'

'I *must* stop her!' Mrs Kranky wailed. 'I can hardly see her as it is!'

'Catch hold of each end and pull,' Mr Kranky said.

By then, Grandma was the size of a match-stick and still shrinking fast.

A moment later, she was no bigger than a pin . . .

Then a pumpkin seed . . .

Then . . .

Then . . .

'Where is she?' cried Mrs Kranky. 'I've lost her!'

'Hooray,' said Mr Kranky.

'She's gone! She's disappeared completely!' cried Mrs Kranky.

'That's what happens to you if you're grumpy and bad-tempered,' said Mr Kranky. 'Great medicine of yours, George.'

George didn't know what to think.

For a few minutes, Mrs Kranky kept wandering round with a puzzled look on her face, saying, 'Mother, where are you? Where've you gone? Where've you got to? How can I find you?' But she calmed down quite quickly. And by lunchtime, she was saying, 'Ah well, I suppose it's all for the best, really. She was a bit of a nuisance around the house, wasn't she?'

'Yes,' Mr Kranky said. 'She most certainly was.'

George didn't say a word. He felt quite trembly. He knew something tremendous had taken place that morning. For a few brief moments he had touched with the very tips of his fingers the edge of a magic world.

There's more to
Roald Dahl
than great stories . . .

Did you know that 10% of author royalties* from this book go
to help the work of the Roald Dahl charities?

Roald Dahl's Marvellous Children's Charity exists to make life better
for seriously ill children because it believes that every child
has the right to a marvellous life.
This marvellous charity helps thousands of children each year
living with serious conditions of the blood and the brain – causes
important to Roald Dahl in his lifetime – whether by providing
nurses, equipment or toys for today's children in the UK, or helping
tomorrow's children everywhere through pioneering research.
Can you do something marvellous to help others?
Find out how at **www.marvellouschildrenscharity.org**

The Roald Dahl Museum and Story Centre, based in Great Missenden
just outside London, is in the Buckinghamshire village where Roald Dahl
lived and wrote. At the heart of the Museum, created to inspire a love of
reading and writing, is his unique archive of letters and manuscripts.
As well as two fun-packed biographical galleries, the Museum boasts an
interactive Story Centre. It is a place for the family, teachers and their
pupils to explore the exciting world of creativity and literacy.
Find out more at **www.roalddahlmuseum.org**

The Roald Dahl's Marvellous Children's Charity (RDMCC) is a registered charity no. 1137409.
The Roald Dahl Museum and Story Centre (RDMSC) is a registered charity no. 1085853.
The Roald Dahl Charitable Trust, a newly established charity,
supports the work of RDMCC and RDMSC.

*Donated royalties are net of commission

ROGUES IN THE GALLERY.

ALAN MOORE (Author and dandy). "They say TODD KLEIN designed this tat and spun his calligraphic skills on it."

KEVIN O'NEILL (Artist and probably Irish). "To be sure, BEN DIMAGMALIW'S colouring gilds the lily an' all."

AMERICAN PUBLISHER (Eavesdropping). "Those foolish fops will work for scraps."

CHRIS STAROS editor	TOP SHELF PRODUCTIONS Chris Staros & Brett Warnock publishers	KNOCKABOUT COMICS Tony Bennett & Josh Palmano publishers	Captain Universe is ©1954 Mic Anglo (used with permission). Special thanks to Iain Sinclair

Visit our online catalogues at www.topshelfcomix.com and www.knockabout.com

1910.

FRATERS AND SORORS...

BELOVED FRATERS AND SORORS...

WE ARE GATHERED IN THE PROFESS-HOUSE.

WE CAN BEGIN.

B-BUT OLIVER...I'M SORRY. I'M SORRY. MASTER...

MASTER, DO WE EVEN KNOW WHAT WE'RE ATTEMPTING TO CALL DOWN? WHAT IF IT'S...?

CALM YOURSELF, ILIEL.

WE WORK ONLY THE LAW. SEE FRATER CYRIL AND FRATER SIMON. DO THEY SEEM AFRAID?

OBSERVE SOROR CYBELE. DOES SHE TREMBLE?

He's right, Soror.

ALL THE MASTER'S TALKING ABOUT IS A CHILD. WHAT COULD BE MORE HARM-LESS?

QUITE. IT'S NOT THE END OF THE WORLD, SOROR ILIEL.

WELL SAID, FRATER CYRIL.

WHAT WE ARE SEEKING TO ESTABLISH HERE IS BUT THE FOUNDING STONE OF OUR INVISIBLE COLLEGE.

A *MOON*-STONE.

A MOON-*CHILD.*

AND ONCE THAT CHILD FULFILLS ITS DESTINY...

...THEN SHALL THE KINGDOMS OF THE EARTH BE PLUNGED INTO A STRANGE AND TERRIBLE NEW AEON.

1: What Keeps Mankind Alive?

ffah!

GET YOUR CLOTHES ON, LASS.

HE WANTS TO SEE YOU.

HELLO, JACK.

ਪ੍ਰਣਾਮ ਬਾਪੂ

ਤੁਹਾਡਾ ਕੀ ਹਾਲ ਐ?

MOBILIS IN MOBIL

EVENIN', MISS JANNI.

ਮੈਂ ਉਂਝ ਈ ਆਂ, ਨਾ ਅੱਗੇ ਤੋਂ ਭੈੜਾ ਨਾ ਚੰਗਾ।

ਮੈਂ ਪੁੱਛਦੀ ਆਂ ਤੁਸੀਂ ਅਪਣਾ ਇਰਾਦਾ ਬਦਲਿਆ ਐ ਜਾਂ ਨਹੀਂ?

ਭੱਲੀ ਨਾ ਹੋ

ਮੈਂ ਹਰਗਿਜ਼ ਨਹੀਂ ਬਦਲਿਆ

ਤੂੰ ਮੇਰੀ ਨਾਫ਼ਰਮਾਨੀ ਕੀਤੀ

ਤੂੰ ਆਪਣੇ ਪਿਓ ਦੀ ਨਾਫ਼ਰਮਾਨੀ ਕੀਤੀ

ਇਹ ਨਾ ਭੁੱਲ ਕਿ ਤੂੰ ਮੇਰੀ ਧੀ ਏਂ

ਨਹੀਂ

ਮੈਂ ਵੀ ਉਹ ਸਾਰੇ ਵਰ੍ਹੇ ਨਹੀਂ ਭੁੱਲੀ ਜਦੋਂ ਤੁਸੀਂ ਉੱਕਾ ਮੇਰੇ ਵੱਲ ਧਿਆਨ ਨਹੀਂ ਕੀਤਾ

ਤੁਸੀਂ ਮੇਰੇ ਵੱਲ ਧਿਆਨ ਇਸ ਲਈ ਨਹੀਂ ਕੀਤਾ ਕਿ ਤੁਹਾਨੂੰ ਪੁੱਤਰ ਚਾਹੀਦਾ ਸੀ

ਆਹੋ, ਮੈਨੂੰ ਪੁੱਤਰ ਚਾਹੀਦਾ ਸੀ ਪਰ, ਮੈਨੂੰ ਤੂੰ ਹੀ ਲੱਭੀ

ਤੇ ਕੀ ਤੂੰ ਮੇਰਾ ਕੰਮ ਤੇ ਮੇਰਾ ਨਾਂ ਅੱਗੇ ਟੋਰੇਂ ਗੀ ?

ਵਾਹ, ਉਹ ਨਾਂ ਕੀ ਜਿਹਦੀ ਕੋਈ ਪਛਾਣ ਨਹੀਂ, ਤੇ ਉਹ ਕੰਮ ਕੀ ਜਿਹੜਾ ਜਾਅਲੀ ਐ ?

ਮੈਂ ਤੇਰੇ ਵਾਂਗ ਜਾਨੂਨੀ ਨਹੀਂ

ਮੇਰੇ ਵੱਲੋਂ ਤੋਂ ਜਹੰਨਮ ਵਿਚ ਜਾ

HEY! CALM DOWN, CAPTAIN. YOU'LL MAKE YOURSELF BAD.

ਤੇਰੀ ਇਹ ਹਿੰਮਤ ਕਿ ਤੂੰ ਮੇਰੇ ਨਾਲ ਇੰਜ ਬੋਲੀਂ ? ਤੈਨੂੰ ਫੈਂਟੀ ਲਵਾਉਣੀ ਚਾਹੀਦੀ ਐ।

≳koff≲ ≳koff≲

Whoa. STEADY ON NOW, YOUNG MISS JANNI.

I'D NEVER HAVE BROUGHT YOU UP HERE IF I'D KNOWN THE CAPTAIN WOULD UPSET YOU...

HE'S NOT A CAPTAIN! WHEN WAS HE IN ANY COUNTRY'S NAVY? HE'S A PRINCE WHO PLAYS WITH BOATS!

DEAR ISHMAEL, PLEASE GET OUT OF MY WAY. I'M NOT IN ANY MOOD TO TALK TO YOU TONIGHT.

WELL, FAIR ENOUGH, CHILD, BUT YOU KNOW YOUR FATHER.

IT MAY BE SOONER OR LATER, BUT HE'LL HAVE HIS WAY.

HE ALWAYS DOES.

FAR AWAY ♪ IN FOREIGN CLIMES, DEAR...

♫ I HAVE ROAMED FOR TWENTY YEARS... ♫

♪ THOUGH THEY'VE THOUGHT ME DEAD AT TIMES, DEAR... ♫♫

FEW HAVE SHED ME ANY TEARS. ♪

:Uuwuhh:

WELL, I SUPPOSE AT LEAST THE MOON IS ABOVE THE YARDARM, SO I'LL PROBABLY JOIN YOU.

WHAT WERE YOU DREAMING ABOUT, ANYWAY? MORE OF THIS OMINOUS STUFF THAT MINA'S SO CONCERNED OVER?

I DON'T KNOW. I ONLY REMEMBER FRAGMENTS: A SINISTER CULT, A FOREIGN GIRL SWIMMING NAKED, SOMEONE SINGING A CATCHY SONG...

PROBABLY NOTHING SIGNIF-ICANT.

GOOD. I'VE NEVER COTTONED TO ALL THIS MYSTICAL TOMMYROT. NO OFFENCE.

NONE TAKEN. IF MY PREMONITIONS OF A DISASTER IN LONDON HADN'T BEEN SO STRONG, I WOULDN'T BE MIXED UP WITH YOU PEOPLE EITHER.

US PEOPLE? DON'T MAKE ME LAUGH, CARNACKI. YOU'RE MORE LIKE THEM THAN I AM.

AFTER ALL, AT LEAST YOU VOLUNTEERED YOUR SERVICES. I WAS BLACK-MAILED INTO THIS WHEN THEY UNCOVERED MY BURGLARY CAREER.

HOW WOULD A DROP OF THE 1736 AMONTILLADO SUIT YOU?

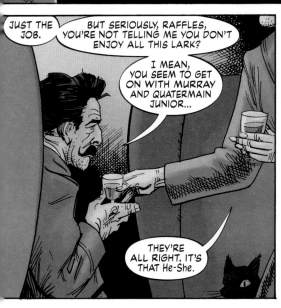

JUST THE JOB.

BUT SERIOUSLY, RAFFLES, YOU'RE NOT TELLING ME YOU DON'T ENJOY ALL THIS LARK?

I MEAN, YOU SEEM TO GET ON WITH MURRAY AND QUATERMAIN JUNIOR...

THEY'RE ALL RIGHT. IT'S THAT He-She.

HA HA. YES, I KNOW WHAT YOU MEAN. THAT WAS A BIT OF A SHOCK FOR ME AS WELL...

TOM...

WHAT WAS A BIT OF A SHOCK? I HOPE IT WAS WORTH WAKING EVERYBODY OVER.

Oh, CARNACKI JUST HAD ONE OF HIS NIGHTMARES. ISN'T THAT RIGHT, TOM?

Really? AND DID IT YIELD ANY CLUES TO OUR FORTHCOMING DISASTER, MR. CARNACKI?

I'M AFRAID NOT...ALTHOUGH THERE WAS SOME STUFF ABOUT A CULT OR SECT OF SOME KIND.

ACTUALLY, THINKING ABOUT IT, ONE OF THE CHAPS I DREAMED OF SEEMED TERRIBLY FAMILIAR...

WHAT A BORE. ALL THE CHAPS I DREAM OF ARE TERRIBLY *OVER*-FAMILIAR.

Oh, LANDO, DO SHUT UP.

SO, MR. CARNACKI, WHERE DID YOU RECOGNISE THE MAN IN YOUR DREAM FROM? SOME FORMER ENEMY, PERHAPS?

NO. HE WAS HOODED, BUT HE LOOKED LIKE SIMON IFF, AN OLD BOY FROM MY CHEYNE WALK CLUB.

THE ONE FULL OF DECADENTS AND OCCULTISTS?

MORNING, EVERYONE. IT IS MORNING, ISN'T IT?

WHAT'S GOING ON?

MR. CARNACKI'S HAD ANOTHER DREAM, THIS ONE ABOUT OCCULTISTS...INCLUDING ONE HE KNOWS, APPARENTLY.

TELL ME, DO YOU THINK THE SECT IN YOUR DREAM MIGHT BE PLOTTING THE DESTRUCTION IN LONDON THAT YOU FORESAW?

I SUPPOSE IT'S POSSIBLE. THEY SEEMED EXCITED ABOUT SOME PROJECT OR SCHEME...

HUH. WELL, I'LL BET LONDON'S SEEN WORSE. DID I EVER TELL YOU ABOUT HOW I HELPED FOUND LONDON? "NEW TROY" WE CALLED IT THEN...

YES, YOU'VE TOLD US. DOZENS OF TIMES, ACTUALLY.

LOOK, THE SCHEME YOU MENTION... COULD IT HAVE ANYTHING TO DO WITH THE IMMINENT CORONATION?

PERHAPS.

I REMEMBER SOMETHING ABOUT USHERING IN A DREADFUL NEW AEON...

Hmm...AND PRESUMABLY NOT THE DREADFUL NEW AEON OF GEORGE THE FIFTH?

I KNOW MILITARY INTELLIGENCE ARE WORRIED ABOUT SOME ANTI-ROYAL PLOT. ALSO, HALLEY'S COMET IS PASSING...

MINA, COME ON. YOU'RE NOT SUPERSTITIOUS, SURELY?

I DIDN'T USED TO BE, MR. RAFFLES. THAT'S WHY I HAVE TO WEAR THIS SCARF.

NO, I THINK A VISIT TO MR. CARNACKI'S CLUB MIGHT BE IN ORDER...

Hmph. I'D BETTER HAVE A SHAVE, THEN.

YOU KNOW, SHAVING EVERY DAY...I ABSOLUTELY HATE IT.

IT'S MUCH MORE TIRESOME THAN HAVING A PERIOD EVERY FEW WEEKS.

Don't you find?

♪ STILL A YOUNG MAN...

♪ ...NOT YET TWENTY...

♪ ...I'D STEP OUT AND TAKE THE AIR.

♪ AS FOR PICKINGS...

♪ ...I HAD PLENTY...

♪ ...MILLER'S COURT TO MITRE SQUARE.

...THINKING ABOUT SIGNING ON FOR CHALLENGER'S EXPEDITION DOWN PERU WAY.

HOW ABOUT YOU?

DUNNO. MIGHT TRAIN AS AN AIRSHIP PILOT. APPARENTLY, THE PAY IS...

LUCKY 'EATHER! LUCKY 'EATHER TO KEEP THE COMET AWAY!

'ERE, DID YOU SEE THE PAPER? IT SAID OLD CUFF 'AD DIED...

WHAT, THE COPPER?

YEAH. 'IM WHAT SOLVED THE MOONSTONE CAPER. HEART ATTACK, SO THE PAPER SAID...

WOTCHER, SUKI. HOW'S TRADE, DEAR?

BRISK. HARDLY STOOD UP ALL NIGHT...

...MARK MY WORDS, BUILDING BIGGER SHIPS MEANS WAR'S COMING. REMEMBER *THE TITAN*...

GET YER LUCKY 'EATHER!

...NEW KING? STUTTERING 'ALF-WIT MORE LIKE...

...ABOUT THAT 14TH EARL OF GURNEY, HIS SPEECH IN THE HOUSE OF LORDS? HE...

CUTTLEFISH HOTE

Staff Wanted

...ALL HALF BARMY. IT'S THEM PUBLIC SCHOOLS, LIKE GREYFRIARS...

LUCKY 'EATHER! GET YER LUCKY CORONATION 'EATHER!

...RUMOUR ABOUT THE CHATTERLYS...

...NEAR QUONG LI'S TEA SHOP IN LIME- HOUSE...

ROLL UP, LADIES AND GENTLEMEN...

'EATHER! KEEP THE COMET AWAY WITH LUCKY 'EATHER!

ROLL UP FOR THE WONDER OF THE AGE! YOU'VE 'EARD ABOUT IT! YOU'VE READ ABOUT IT!

IT TERRORIZED THE 'IGH SEAS! IT BROUGHT DOWN THE BARNES BRIDGE MARTIAN!

NOW 'ERE IT IS, LADIES AND GENTS, BEFORE YOUR VERY EYES...

AH, HELLO THERE. IT'S THOMAS CARNACKI. I'M HERE FOR THE MERLIN SOCIETY MEETING.

MR. CARNACKI. OF COURSE.

AND YOUR FRIENDS?

OH, I'M SORRY. THIS IS MISS MURRAY AND MIS...MISTER ORLANDO, WHILE THIS IS MISTER QUATERMAIN, THE SON OF THE ADVENTURER.

THEY'RE MY GUESTS.

INDEED. PLEASE STEP THIS WAY.

INCIDENTALLY, MR. QUATERMAIN, I GREATLY ADMIRED YOUR FATHER. A TRAGIC LOSS.

YES. YES, IT WAS. THANK YOU.

NOT AT ALL, SIR.

YOUR COAT, MADAM?

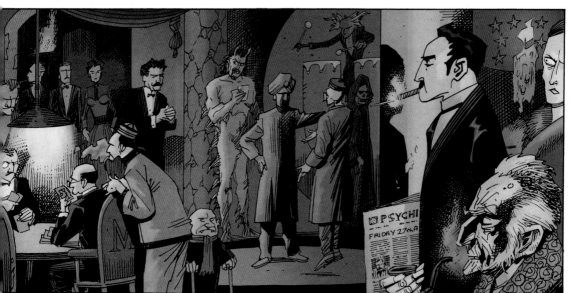

Hmph. RUM-OOKING CROWD, I MUST SAY.

ALLAN, DON'T BE SO PROVINCIAL.

SO, MR. CARNACKI, ARE THESE ALL OCCULTISTS?

YES, OR INVESTIGATORS OF THE UNEARTHLY. THAT'S DYSON AND PHILLIPS, AND THERE'S DEAR OLD JOHNNY SILENCE...

THE FELLOW IN THE TURBAN TALKING TO DR. TAVERNER, THAT'S PRINCE ZALESKI.

I CAN'T SEE OLD IFFY ANY-WHERE...

NEVER MIND. HOPEFULLY, A.J. IS GATHERING INTELLI-GENCE AT THIS MOMENT.

Hmm. FIRST TIME FOR EVERYTHING, I SUPPOSE.

LOOK, MINA, SINCE I KNOW IFFY, WHY DON'T ALLAN AND I LOOK FOR HIM?

YOU AND ORLANDO COULD MINGLE...

...AND PRY. GOOD IDEA.

YOU KNOW, I THINK A FORMER DOCTOR OF MINE USED TO COME HERE...

OH, LOOK! THERE'S SOME-ONE *I* KNOW.

THIS IS GETTING INTEREST-ING.

IFF, Simon Alexander

EXCUSE ME, MR. ZANONI, ISN'T IT?

MY, um, MOTHER WAS IN FORTUNIO'S ENTOURAGE TO SEE YOUR "RITE OF SMARRA."

FORTUNIO, EH? A TRUE GENTLEMAN.

FORTUNIO HAD MET THEM ALL: THE SICILIAN, THE COUNT VON OST. ALL THE GREATS.

Mm. FASCINAT-ING.

ACTUALLY, WE WERE LOOKING FOR A SIMON IFF...

Huh. YOU'RE NOT FRIENDS OF HIS, I HOPE?

IFF'S A SCOUNDREL. HE SIDED AGAINST ME IN MY MAGICAL WAR.

HE SIDED WITH *HADDO.*

OLIVER HADDO, THE DIABOLIST? DIDN'T HE DIE IN STAFFORDSHIRE A COUPLE OF YEARS AGO?

LET'S HOPE SO.

REPORTEDLY, HADDO WAS ATTEMPTING TO MAKE HOMUNCULI.

HOMUNCULI? WHY?

ISN'T IT OBVIOUS? HE NEEDS MOONCHILD TO END THE WORLD.

MINA?

I'M AFRAID WE'VE DRAWN A BLANK.

SHALL WE BE GOING?

NICELY TIMED, TOM. A.J. SHOULD BE FINISHED BY NOW.

Mm. AND NOBODY HAS SEEN IFFY IN WEEKS.

LOTS OF GLOOMY TALK, THOUGH.

GLOOMY? IN WHAT WAY?

IN AN OCCULT WAY. IMMINENT DOOMSDAY FORECASTS AND THE LIKE, CONNECTED WITH THE CORONATION...

I SAY! FANCY MEETING YOU HERE.

FANCY. DID YOU FIND IFF'S FILE?

PIECE OF CAKE. I'VE GOT IT HERE.

HOW ABOUT YOU LOT? DID YOU FIND OUT ANYTHING?

NOTHING VERY CHEERFUL, I'M AFRAID.

OMINOUS THINGS ARE HAPPENING, AT LEAST ACCORDING TO PSYCHIC RUMOUR.

HAPPENING AS WE SPEAK.

Ishmael?

Oh, GOD. IS HE **BAD,** JACK?

I KNEW IT'D FINISH HIM, HER VANISHING LIKE THAT...

YOU'D BEST COME AND SEE FOR YOURSELF.

MOBILIS IN MOBILI

ALL MY OLD HAUNTS, THEY REMIND ME...

...OF THE GIRLS I KNEW BACK THEN.

POOR AND HAPLESS...

...LEFT BEHIND ME...

...NEVER TO BE...

...MET AGAIN.

You gentlemen can peek while she's slinging out the slops...

...and she's slinging out the slops as you're peeking. ♪

♪ Or you meet her in the hallway and you wink as you pass... ♪

...and you make some smart remark about her titties or her arse...

...but you'll never know to whom you're speaking. ♪

♪ You have no IDEA to whom you are speaking. ♪

He's
dead.

Hmm.

SO, BASICALLY, THEY'RE HOLDING A SÉANCE, THEN.

NO ENTRY

PRETTY MUCH.

MINA'S STILL WORRIED ABOUT THOSE OCCULTISTS IN CARNACKI'S VISION.

WELL, THE FOLDER I PINCHED SAID IFF KNOCKED AROUND WITH THAT SATANIST CHAP.

OLIVER HADDO. YES, IT SAID THEY'D BEEN CONNECTED.

BUT HADDO DIED TWO YEARS AGO, IN A FIRE...

YES, SUPPOSEDLY. IT'S A MURKY BUSINESS.

IT USUALLY IS WITH MINA.

COME ON. DO YOU FANCY STRETCHING YOUR LEGS?

I'LL SAY.

SHE WAS ORIGINALLY YOUR DAD'S COMPANION, WASN'T SHE?

Mm? Oh. Oh, Mina. Yes. Yes, she was.

WE THOUGHT WE'D KEEP HER IN THE FAMILY.

Ha. DON'T BLAME YOU.

WHAT ABOUT ORLANDO?

ORLANDO? WHAT DO YOU MEAN?

WELL, YOU KNOW. ALL THAT STUFF ABOUT POSING FOR THE MONA LISA AND WHAT-NOT.

IS HE BARMY?

DON'T LET HIM HEAR YOU SAY THAT.

WHETHER THAT'S SWORD'S EXCALIBUR OR NOT, HE'S AWFULLY GOOD WITH IT.

Is he... close to you two?

ALL DUE RESPECT, RAFFLES, THAT'S NONE OF YOUR BLOODY BUSINESS.

NO. NO, I SUPPOSE NOT. SORRY.

I'M JUST RATHER ON EDGE AT THE MOMENT.

Huh. CARNACKI'S DOOMSDAY PREDICTIONS GETTING TO YOU, ARE THEY?

IT'S NOT SO MUCH THAT.

I'M MORE WORRIED ABOUT THE PROSPECT OF A WAR.

WOULD YOU FIGHT?

I'D FEEL OBLIGED TO. I'VE BEEN A BIT OF A ROTTER OVER THE YEARS, QUATER-MAIN.

STILL, EVERYBODY DIES EVENTUALLY, EH?

Yes. YES, I SUPPOSE THEY DO.

WELL, MR. CARNACKI? ARE YOU GETTING ANY INFORMATION ABOUT IFF OR HADDO FROM YOUR... WHAT DID YOU CALL IT?

IT'S A SCRYING GLASS, A BLACK MIRROR MADE OF OBSIDIAN.

IT'S FROM THE MUSEUM'S COLLECTION. IT USED TO BELONG TO GLORIANA'S ALCHEMIST, JOHN SUBTLE.

OH, HONESTLY! SUBTLE WAS JUST A CODE-NAME THAT QUEEN GLORY GAVE TO DUKE PROSPERO OF MILAN. I WAS THERE.

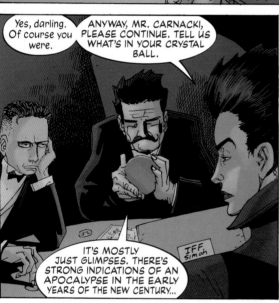

YES, DARLING. OF COURSE YOU WERE.

ANYWAY, MR. CARNACKI, PLEASE CONTINUE. TELL US WHAT'S IN YOUR CRYSTAL BALL.

IT'S MOSTLY JUST GLIMPSES. THERE'S STRONG INDICATIONS OF AN APOCALYPSE IN THE EARLY YEARS OF THE NEW CENTURY...

AREN'T THERE ALWAYS? YOU DO MEAN THIS CURRENT CENTURY, I TAKE IT?

I PRESUME SO.

I'M GETTING MUDDLED VISIONS OF KING'S CROSS, AND A HOTEL ON THE DOCK-SIDE. THERE'S HUMAN HEADS PILED UP. IT'S TERRIBLE.

I SEE. AND ARE SIMON IFF OR OLIVER HADDO INVOLVED IN ANY OF THIS?

YES. YES, I SENSE THEY'RE MIXED UP IN THE APOCALYPSE PART OF THE VISION.

I ALSO CONNECT THEM WITH KING'S CROSS.

"KING'S CROSS." THAT IS THE RAILWAY STATION, I SUPPOSE, AND NOT AN OBLIQUE REFERENCE TO THE IMMINENT CORONATION?

HM. I HADN'T THOUGHT OF THAT. THE WAY DIVINATION WORKS, IT COULD BE ALLUD-ING TO BOTH THINGS.

THAT SOUNDS OMINOUS.

WHAT ABOUT THIS HOTEL ON THE DOCKS YOU MENTIONED?

THAT'S MORE INDISTINCT.

I SENSE SOME THREAT...A RUTHLESS KILLER RECENTLY ARRIVED IN ENGLAND...SOME CRISIS ERUPTING ON CORONATION DAY. NOTHING SPECIFIC, THOUGH.

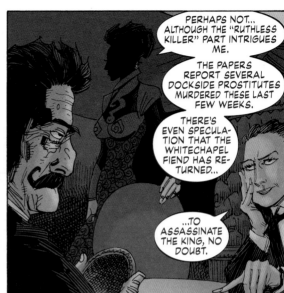

PERHAPS NOT... ALTHOUGH THE "RUTHLESS KILLER" PART INTRIGUES ME.

THE PAPERS REPORT SEVERAL DOCKSIDE PROSTITUTES MURDERED THESE LAST FEW WEEKS.

THERE'S EVEN SPECULA- TION THAT THE WHITECHAPEL FIEND HAS RE- TURNED...

...TO ASSASSINATE THE KING, NO DOUBT.

WELL, WHY NOT? IT'S SCARCELY MORE RIDICULOUS THAN YOU HAVING HIGH TEA WITH PROSPERO AND QUEEN GLORIANA.

OH, COME ON! IT'S A BIT ELABORATE, SURELY? AND WHERE DO THESE KING'S CROSS BLACK MAGICIANS FIT IN?

THEY MAY NOT FIT IN AT ALL. ON THE OTHER HAND, THEIR RITUALS MAY BE CAUSING ALL OF THESE EVENTS.

THANK YOU, MR. CARNACKI.

I PROPOSE WE INVESTIGATE KING'S CROSS...AFTER INFORMING MILITARY INTELLIGENCE, NATURALLY.

OH, BLAST! DOES THAT MEAN WE HAVE TO SIT THROUGH A MEETING WITH FATTY HOLMES?

WELL, NOT ALL OF US, SURELY?

BESIDES, HOLMES MIGHT HAVE USEFUL INFORMATION. ONE MEETING'S HARDLY THE END OF THE WORLD.

Hm.

YES, WELL.

LET'S HOPE NOT, ANYWAY.

I...I DIDN'T THINK HE'D EVER REALLY DIE.

I DON'T KNOW HOW I FEEL. WE DIDN'T EVEN LIKE EACH OTHER...

THAT'S NOT TRUE.

BLESS YOU, MISS, YOU WERE ALL HE LIVED FOR.

WHEN YOU RUN OFF, HIS HEART BROKE.

HE WANTED A SUCCESSOR, ISHMAEL. NOT A DAUGHTER.

Aye, well...

TO TELL THE TRUTH, MISS JANNI, THAT WAS ONE OF THE THINGS I'D COME HERE TO TALK TO YOU ABOUT.

WHAT?

ISHMAEL, HOW *COULD* YOU? YOU KNOW I'LL NEVER AGREE. IT WAS WHY I RAN AWAY IN THE FIRST PLACE...

HEAR ME OUT, MISS...

IT WAS HIS DYING WISH. HE ASKED ME TO...TO MAKE SOME CHANGES TO THE NAUTILUS, THEN GIVE IT TO YOU.

NO, ISHMAEL!

I DON'T WANT IT! I DON'T WANT TO BE A FANATIC!

ANYWAY, I'VE MADE A NEW LIFE HERE...

NOT MUCH OF ONE, THOUGH.

YOU...YOU CAN'T SAY THAT. I'M... I'M GETTING ON WELL. I'M RESPECTED.

RESPECTED?

JANNI, YOU COULD BE OUR **QUEEN.** JUST SAY THE WORD, LASS.

Ishmael, I'm not...

MISS JANNI. I'M BEGGING YOU. I NEED A CAPTAIN, MISS. WE ALL DO.

LOOK, AT LEAST TAKE THIS FLARE GUN.

FLARE GUN...?

FOR IF YOU CHANGE YOUR MIND. THE NAUTILUS IS MOORED IN THE THAMES ESTUARY.

IF YOU EVER WANT US, MISS, JUST...

NO! HAVEN'T YOU BEEN LISTENING TO ME?

GET OUT, ISHMAEL! GET OUT AND LEAVE ME ALONE!

M-MISS, JANNI, PLEASE...

ISHMAEL, JUST **GO!**

I WON'T CHANGE MY MIND. YOU **KNOW** THAT, IF YOU KNOW ANYTHING ABOUT ME.

AYE, MISS. I RECKON I DO.

YOU'RE STUBBORN.

JUST LIKE YOUR FATHER.

NO VISITORS SPITTING DRINK DOGS

More tea?

Yes, yes, thank you, we will.

Splendid.

Bond? More tea for our guests, if you would.

Does...does madam require milk with her tea?

Oh, yes please. Just a splash would be lovely.

So, to business. What of Carnacki's visions?

Well, they're imprecise, but partly they concern a murderer, recently arrived on London's docksides.

Hmm. Yes, the MacHeath case.

We're already studying that.

MacHeath?

John MacHeath, a merchant navy captain recently returned from Argentina.

He left England in 1888, the year of the Whitechapel slayings.

Bloody hell.

Well, quite.

He's also a direct descendant of MacHeath the 18th century highwayman.

A police inspector, "Tiger" Brown, is currently looking into it.

I see.

Actually, Mr. Carnacki thought one occult source might be behind all of these events.

This would be the sect you mentioned?

YES. THE HADDO CULT. OUR ASSOCIATE MR. RAFFLES ACQUIRED INFORMATION LINKING A SUSPECT OF OURS WITH HADDO.

WELL, OF COURSE, MR. HADDO IS OFFICIALLY DEAD...

...ALTHOUGH HIS MAGICAL ORDER HAS SURVIVED HIM.

I THINK THEIR "PROFESS-HOUSE" OR WHATEVER IT'S CALLED IS NEAR KING'S CROSS.

Really? THAT'S INTERESTING.

KING'S CROSS FEATURED IN CARNACKI'S VISIONS. DO WE HAVE YOUR LEAVE TO INVESTIGATE?

I SUPPOSE SO.

YOU SHOULD CONSULT MR. NORTON FIRST, THOUGH.

NORTON? YOU MEAN ANDREW NORTON, THE PRISONER OF LONDON?

YES. HE'S GOOD WITH THE OCCULT STUFF AND DUE TO MATERIALIZE AT KING'S CROSS SOON, APPARENTLY.

BESIDES, I BELIEVE HE WORKED WITH YOUR PREDECESSORS.

INCIDENTALLY, HOW WAS MY BROTHER WHEN YOU VISITED HIM LAST?

HE'S WELL.

H-He sends regards.

Haha!

MY DEAR MISS MURRAY AND MR. QUATERMAIN... JUNIOR.

IT'S ALWAYS A PLEASURE, EVEN WHEN I KNOW YOU'RE LYING.

PLEASE, SHOW YOURSELVES OUT.

CUTTLEFISH HOTEL

♪ You patrons of the house try to treat her like a louse...

♪ ...and you think she doesn't know what you're trying.

♪ While she's clearing your leftovers you'll suggest she needs a man...

♪ ...Whereas I suggest you eat, drink, and be merry as you can...

...because tomorrow's soon enough for dying.

Tomorrow we could ALL be dying.

WELL, FIRSTLY, WHEN ORLANDO'S MALE HE RATHER IRRITATES ME.

SECONDLY, HE'S MORE USEFUL WITH ALLAN AND CARNACKI, INVESTIGATING THIS NEARBY CULT HEADQUARTERS, SO...HANG ON.

CAN YOU FEEL THAT PRESSURE IN YOUR EARS?

I THINK IT MEANS NORTON'S ALMOST HERE...

£50 REWARD

GEORGE.M PLUMMER

the Beast

NEW RIPPER HORRORS

SCOTLAND

1/

Blimey.

M-MINA, IS THIS GOING TO BE ALL RIGHT? MY HAIR'S STANDING UP ON END...

I...I DON'T KNOW. I HAVEN'T FELT ANYTHING REMOTELY LIKE THIS SINCE ALLAN AND I WERE IN ARKHAM.

TH-THIS SENSATION THAT SOMETHING IS JUST ABOUT TO...

GREAT NORT

RAILWA

GREATNOR1

...break through...

HI. How are you?

Um..."hi." W-WE'RE VERY WELL, THANK YOU.

Y-YOU MUST BE ANDREW NORTON. THIS IS ANTHONY RAFFLES AND I'M MINA MURRAY.

GASLIGHT UNDER-STUDIES.

MARVELLOUS.

Uh... YOU KNOW OF US, THEN?

OF COURSE. COFFINS AT CARFAX, BLOOD FOR OIL. PATRICK KEILLER MAPPING THE MARTIANS' CRATER.

DEAD TRAILS. ABANDONED PANICS.

I...I see.

ACTUALLY, MR. NORTON, WE WERE HOPING YOU COULD INFORM US CONCERNING ONE OLIVER HADDO, AND ALSO CERTAIN ACTIVITIES CENTRED ON KING'S CROSS...

HADDO? CROWLEY MANQUÉ. THE GREAT BEAST REFLECTED IN AN OVER-POLISHED OCCASIONAL TABLE. KING'S CROSS, THOUGH... I'D ADVISE YOU TO BE CAREFUL.

THE PLACE IS A MYTH-SUMP, INVITES APOCALYPTIC THINKING. DANGEROUS AGENDAS HURRYING TO MAKE THEIR CONNECTION.

APOCALYPTIC? HOW DO YOU MEAN?

ISN'T IT OBVIOUS? JULY SEVENTH. PARADISE BACKPACKERS.

A CONSTELLATION OF CIGARETTE BURNS ON ARCHER'S BACK. THE STARS ARE RIGHT.

MISPLACED MEMORIALS. FOR-GOTTEN FIRES. RIMBAUD, VERLAINE, LYRIC GREASE. BOADICEA'S URBAN LEGEND UNDER PLATFORM TEN.

A QUARTER PLATFORM OVER, THE FRANCHISE EXPRESS, GATHERING STEAM.

Anyway...

♪ It must have got you hard when you had her in the yard...

...but you've no idea how hard things are getting. ♪

♪ And you think of what you've done as you're buttoning your flies...

♪ Of an act so bloody shameful you can't look me in the eyes... ♪

♪ ...and which you imagine you're regretting. ♪

♪ Believe me, you don't **KNOW** regretting. ♪

ORLANDO, MISS MURRAY SAID WE SHOULD OBSERVE THIS PLACE, NOT BREAK IN.

YES, WELL. FRANKLY, CARNACKI, MINA CAN SOMETIMES BE RATHER UN-ADVENTUROUS.

I'LL TELL HER YOU SAID THAT, AND YOU'LL BE LOSING YOUR BALLS EARLIER THAN YOU EXPECTED.

OH, COME ON, ALLAN. WHERE'S THE HARM?

I MEAN, RAFFLES IS *ALWAYS* BREAKING AND ENTERING. SHE DOESN'T MIND *HIM.*

Hm. D'YOU THINK HE FANCIES HER?

LOOK, CAN WE JUST *DO* THIS?

ALL RIGHT, CARNACKI, DON'T GET IN A FUNK.

I'M NO RAFFLES, EVIDENTLY, BUT I WAS ONCE *VERY* CLOSE TO SINBAD.

PEGO LIKE A STALLION'S...

...AND THE MOST INGENIOUS THIEF OF THE EIGHTH CENTURY.

Ah.

THERE WE GO.

I--I CAN'T SAY I LIKE THE ATMOSPHERE.

HE'S GOT A POINT, LANDO. IF I'D KNOWN WE WERE BREAKING IN I'D HAVE BROUGHT A GUN.

OH, DO DRY UP, THE PAIR OF YOU.

WHO NEEDS GUNS WHEN I'M HERE WITH MY FABLED BLADE?

LANDO, THAT SWORD ISN'T EXCALIBUR.

YES IT *IS*. AND I HAD TO SUBDUE THE *REAL* LADY OF THE LAKE...A TERRIFYING UNDINE...IN ORDER TO GRAB IT.

FELLOWS, PLEASE...

I THINK YOU SHOULD BE TAKING THIS MORE SERIOUSLY.

WHAT IF OLIVER HADDO REALLY IS STILL ALIVE?

SURELY, HADDO WAS JUST A FRAUD?

OF COURSE HE WAS.

BELIEVE ME, DEAR, AFTER YOU'VE KNOWN MERLIN, FAUST AND PROSPERO, THEY'RE *ALL* FRAUDS.

YES, WELL. LET'S HOPE YOU'RE RIGHT.

OF COURSE I'M RIGHT.

MODERN OCCULTISTS ARE ALL TALK.

PROSPERO HAD MORE POWER IN HIS LITTLE FINGER THAN THEY'VE GOT IN THEIR...

...entire...

Gentlemen...

...WON'T YOU COME IN?

GOOD GOD.

MINA, LOOK AT THAT.

IT LOOKS LIKE IT'S OVER THE EAST END.

YES. YES, IT DOES. LET'S ASK THIS BOBBY IF HE KNOWS ANYTHING.

CONSTABLE? EXCUSE ME...

I'M WILHELMINA MURRAY. WE'RE WITH MILITARY INTELLIGENCE. DO YOU KNOW WHAT THAT FLARE IS IN AID OF?

WELL, MISS, THEY'VE POSSIBLY CAPTURED MacHEATH.

MacHEATH THE DOCKSIDE MURDERER?

THAT'S HIM. IF TIGER BROWN'S COLLARED MacHEATH, THAT FLARE COULD BE THE TARTS CELE-BRATING.

I HEAR HE'LL HANG BEFORE DAWN.

BEFORE DAWN? THAT'S A BIT HASTY, ISN'T IT?

IT'S WHAT YOUR INTELLIGENCE PEOPLE ORDERED, I'M TOLD.

ANYWAY, I'D BEST BE GETTING ON.

EVENING, ALL.

MINA, IS THERE SOMETHING GOING ON HERE THAT WE'RE MISSING?

VERY POSSIBLY.

COME ON. LET'S RECALL ALLAN AND THE OTHERS FROM THEIR SURVEILLANCE MISSION...

...BEFORE WE GET IN DEEPER OVER OUR HEADS THAN WE ALREADY ARE.

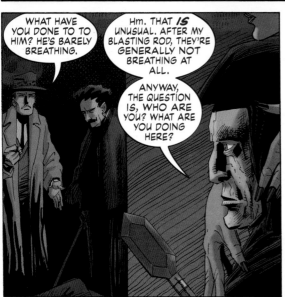

WHAT HAVE YOU DONE TO TO HIM? HE'S BARELY BREATHING.

Hm. THAT **IS** UNUSUAL. AFTER MY BLASTING ROD, THEY'RE GENERALLY NOT BREATHING AT ALL.

ANYWAY, THE QUESTION IS, WHO ARE YOU? WHAT ARE YOU DOING HERE?

I KNOW THE OLDER FELLOW FROM MY CLUB, MASTER. HE'S CARNACKI. CARNACKI THE GHOST FINDER.

OH...THE WHISTLING ROOM CAPER? I'VE HEARD OF YOU.

AND I OF YOU.

YOU ARE OLIVER HADDO, I TAKE IT?

WHAT? ME? OF COURSE NOT. HADDO'S DEAD. HADN'T YOU HEARD?

I'M DR. KARSWELL TRELAWNEY, VARIOUSLY OF STONEDENE, AND LUFFORD IN WARWICKSHIRE.

FRATER SIMON YOU APPARENTLY KNOW ALREADY. THIS IS SOROR CYBELE, AND THERE'S FRATER CYRIL.

YES. YES, IT'S EXACTLY AS IT WAS IN MY DREAM, EXCEPT...

EXCEPT THERE WAS ANOTHER WOMAN. SOME ONE CALLED "ILIEL."

NEVER HEARD OF HER.

ILIEL, THOUGH... THE NAME ADDS UP TO EIGHTY-ONE. A LUNAR NUMBER.

LUNAR...I REMEMBER NOW. IN MY DREAM YOU WERE PLANNING TO CREATE SOMETHING CALLED A MOONCHILD...

REALLY? WELL, DREAMS CAN BE NONSENSE. I ASSURE YOU, I'VE CURRENTLY NO SUCH PLAN.

WE ARE SIMPLE OCCULT SCHOLARS.

THE MASTER'S RIGHT. WE MERELY REPRESENT AN INVISIBLE COLLEGE.

ABSOLUTELY. WE'RE RATHER LIKE THE ROSICRUCIANS. WE GATHER IN OUR "HOUSE OF PROFESSORS" TO WORSHIP.

SO, MR. CARNACKI, PERHAPS YOUR PORTENTOUS VISIONS WERE MISTAKEN?

ON THE OTHER HAND, IT'S CONCEIVABLE THAT THEY SIMPLY HAVEN'T HAPPENED YET.

NOW, PERHAPS YOU'D TAKE YOUR DISHY YOUNG FRIEND AND LEAVE...

...BEFORE HE FINDS HIMSELF ON THE WRONG END OF MY *OTHER* BLASTING ROD.

YOU FILTHY BLOODY SWINE...

...gluhh...

COME ON, QUATERMAIN. DON'T LET HIM RILE YOU.

I DOUBT THERE'S ANOTHER CHARGE IN THAT MAGIC WAND OF HIS, BUT THERE'S NO SENSE US FINDING OUT THE HARD WAY...

WELL, NOW, FRATER CYRIL. THERE'S A SIGN FROM THE GODS IF EVER I SAW ONE.

EVIDENTLY WE SHOULD LOCATE SOMEONE TO BE THIS "SOROR ILIEL"...

...AND ONLY *THEN* SHOULD WE COMMENCE OUR MOONCHILD.

oh, FOR GOD'S SAKE!

WHAT THE BLOODY HELL HAPPENED TO HIM?

he...HE WAS BLASTED WITH HADDO'S WAND.

w-WE'RE PRETTY SURE IT WAS HADDO...

HADDO? WHAT WERE YOU DOING CONFRONTING HADDO, YOU IDIOTS?

YOU WERE SUPPOSED TO BE ON A SURVEILLANCE MISSION!

WELL, YOU SEE, ORLANDO SAID...

ORLANDO? AND DO YOU TAKE INSTRUCTIONS FROM THIS...THIS DELUSIONAL TROLLOP, OR FROM ME?

m-MINA, DEAR HEART, I AM ACTUALLY PRESENT, YOU KNOW.

I DON'T CARE! THIS GROUP IS A SHAMBLES!

DARE I ASK IF YOU LEARNED ANYTHING VALUABLE?

COME ON, DARLING. WE DID OUR BEST...

DON'T "DARLING" ME. AND I TAKE IT THE ANSWER TO MY QUESTION IS "NO?"

th-THE CULT AREN'T PLANNING ANYTHING. I-IT WASN'T LIKE MY DREAM...

I SEE. SO ALL THIS HAS BEEN POINTLESS.

AND THAT'S *OUR* FAULT, IS IT? WHAT ABOUT YOU?

DID THIS NORTON TELL YOU ANY- THING?

Th-THAT ISN'T THE ISSUE.

AT LEAST WE LEARNED MACHEATH IS TO BE HUNG AT DAWN TOMORROW.

WHAT? HOLMES DIDN'T TELL US ABOUT THAT...

NO, HE DIDN'T. I SUGGEST WE LOCATE THE PROPOSED EXECUTION SITE AND FIND OUT WHY.

THIS TEAM'S USELESS. WE NEED TO GET A GRIP ON THINGS.

Mm.

WELL, PERHAPS IF WE HAD BETTER LEADERSHIP WE MIGHT NOT SPEND OUR TIME RUNNING IN CIRCLES.

NOW, WHEN I WAS ALEXANDER'S ADVISOR...

OH! THAT IS THE ABSOLUTE LIMIT!

LISTEN, YOU CAN HAVE THE DOUBLE BED TO YOURSELVES TONIGHT. I'M SLEEPING DOWNSTAIRS.

Mina! Don't tell the neighbourhood...

OH, SHUT UP! I'LL BE AT MACHEATH'S EXECUTION.

UNLESS YOUR NEW STRATEGIST CONCOCTS A BETTER PLAN, I EXPECT I'LL SEE YOU THERE.

MINA...

WELL, THAT'S TORN IT.

LANDO, THAT HAS TO BE THE MOST STUPID THING YOU'VE EVER SAID.

OH, I DON'T KNOW. THERE WAS, "OH LOOK! WHAT A WONDERFUL HORSE!"

THAT WAS AT TROY.

As morning gently breaks, all you libertines and rakes can congratulate yourselves on your fast one.

When she walks into the lobby you look hurriedly away...

...and pretend to be concerned about the matters of the day...

...as engrossed as if it were your last one.

We never know which one's our last one.

She sits there calm while outside there's alarm, and you have your first moment of doubt...

...when you notice that she's smiling through her bruises...

...and you think, "Christ, what's **she** got to smile about?"

...and the **ship**, the **black raider**, is announced on the wharfside...

...by a scream from without.

MR. HOLMES. THERE YOU ARE.

WOULD YOU MIND TELLING ME WHAT'S GOING ON?

NOT AT ALL. IT'S AN EXECUTION. WE'RE HANGING MacHEATH.

WITH RESPECT, SIR, I KNOW THAT. BUT WHY SO HURRIEDLY? IS THERE TO BE NO TRIAL?

OF COURSE NOT. IT MIGHT EMBARRASS THE ARISTOCRACY.

THE ARISTOCRACY? WHAT DO THEY HAVE TO DO WITH ANYTHING?

MY DEAR LADY, THIS IS ENGLAND. THEY HAVE TO DO WITH EVERYTHING...

...ESPECIALLY 1888'S NOTORIOUS WHITECHAPEL MURDERS.

YOU SEE, MacHEATH ABSCONDED FOR ARGENTINA IN EARLY DECEMBER THAT YEAR.

THE LAST MURDER HAPPENED ON BOXING DAY.

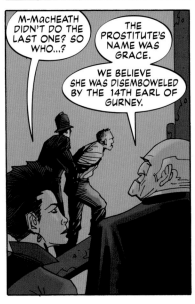

M-MacHEATH DIDN'T DO THE LAST ONE? SO WHO...?

THE PROSTITUTE'S NAME WAS GRACE.

WE BELIEVE SHE WAS DISEMBOWELED BY THE 14TH EARL OF GURNEY.

BETTER EVERYONE THINKS MacHEATH DID THEM ALL, eh? A TRIAL WOULD ONLY RAISE AWKWARD QUESTIONS.

INCIDENTALLY, HOW DID YOUR PREDICTED ARMAGEDDON TURN OUT?

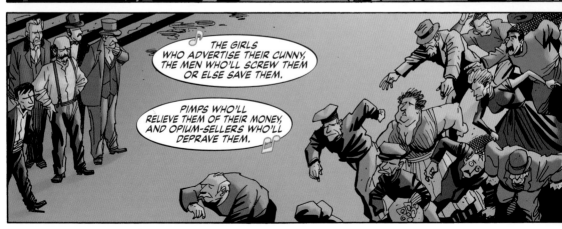

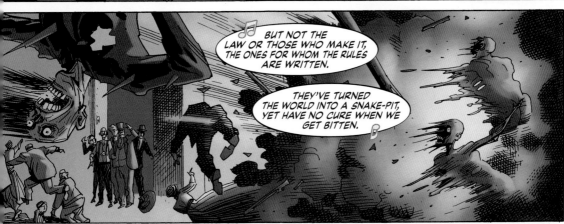

SO, THEN...

IF MR. MacHEATH HAS NO FURTHER LESSONS OR MORAL INSTRUCTIONS FOR US, LET US PROCEED WITH...

M, WAIT! Th-THERE'S A COURIER, SIR. FROM WHITE-HALL...

WHAT?

I-IT'S A MESSAGE CONCERNING THE EARL OF GURNEY, SIR.

Y-YOU BETTER READ IT YOURSELF...

DEAR SUFFERING CHRIST.

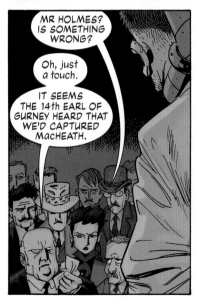

MR HOLMES? IS SOMETHING WRONG?

Oh, just a touch.

IT SEEMS THE 14th EARL OF GURNEY HEARD THAT WE'D CAPTURED MacHEATH.

HIS LORDSHIP DIDN'T LIKE THE THOUGHT OF HIS PRIZE KILL BEING TAKEN AWAY FROM HIM, APPARENTLY.

HE'S CONFESSED TO ALL THE WHITECHAPEL MURDERS.

IT'S SIMPLY TOO BAD.

I MEAN, WHAT MORE COULD POSSIBLY GO WRONG?

Um...WELL, ACTUALLY, SIR, THE COURIER SAID SOMETHING ELSE...

WHAT? YOU IMBECILE, WHY DIDN'T YOU TELL ME?

I-IT WASN'T PART OF HIS MESSAGE, SIR.

IT WAS SOMETHING HE HEARD ON HIS WAY HERE...

I-IT'S THE EAST END, SIR.

IT'S UNDER ATTACK BY A WARSHIP.

MY GOD. MY GOD...

O-ORGANIZE THE MILITARY. GET THEM TO THE AREA AT ONCE.

SIR, MY PEOPLE COULD BE THERE MUCH MORE QUICKLY...

YES. GOOD IDEA.

AND YOU PREDICTED A RUTHLESS KILLER ON THE WATERFRONT, DIDN'T YOU?

WHAT A SHAME WE ALL THOUGHT IT WAS MR. MacHEATH.

YOU HEARD HIM, EVERYONE. LET'S FLAG DOWN A COACH AND GET OVER TO THE DOCKS...

wh-WHAT SHOULD WE DO ABOUT MacHEATH, SIR?

YOU MEAN NOW THAT GURNEY'S CONFESSED EVEN TO MURDERS COMMITTED WHILE HE WAS IN THE MADHOUSE?

WE LET HIM GO, I EXPECT.

R-RELEASE MacHEATH, SIR?

WHY NOT?

IT SEEMS THAT IN OUR NEW CENTURY, FORTUNE IS SET TO FAVOUR MR. MacHEATH AND HIS KIND...

...AND MAY HEAVEN HELP US ALL.

♪ Now you think your leg is broke, and you're crawling through the smoke, and a hundred bloody pirates are landing...

...and their shells have blown the roofs off and demolished every wall, and there's just this one old hotel that they haven't touched at all...

♪ ...so you ask, "Why is that still standing?"

And you ask, "Why is *that* one standing?"

Maybe they've heard, by some sign or some word, there's a grand Lord or Lady living here...

...and then you see her stepping out into the sunlight, with her hair down, and a rose behind her ear...

...and the **ship**, the **black raider**, hoists a flag up its masthead and gives a great cheer.

You can't see the sun at all for a choking, smoky pall and the light upon the river is sickly...

...and someone says, "We've had it," and you privately concur because they're rounding up the hostages and dragging them to her, asking her...

KILL THEM SLOW, OR QUICKLY?

Asking *her*, "Kill them slow, or quickly?"

Over the quay it's as quiet as can be, just faint groans and the slop of the tide.

She'll consider a while, then decide...

KILL THEM SLOW.

And as the heads mount, she'll just smile and say...

Huh.

NEXT TIME YOU'LL KNOW ME.

And the **ship**, the **black raider**, full of plunder and glee...

...prepares for the sea.

GOD, THIS IS HAVOC.

EXCUSE ME, WE'RE AGENTS OF THE CROWN. WHAT ON EARTH'S GOING ON?

LET ME BY! IT'S PIRATES! *HUNDREDS* OF THEM!

PIRATES? WAS HE JOKING? THIS IS THE TWENTIETH CENTURY...

YES. YES, IT IS, ISN'T IT? I KEEP FORGET-TING.

COME ON. LET'S LOOK DOWN...

...HERE...

I--I DON'T BELIEVE THIS. HALF OF THE DOCKSIDE IS...WELL, IT'S GONE. AND THERE'RE PIRATES *EVERYWHERE*...

GOSH. I LIKE THE SOUND OF THAT.

CHRIST, ORLANDO, DON'T. NOT ON YOUR OWN...

Oh, HUSH. THIS IS THE BLADE OF ENGLAND'S GREATEST DEFENDER.

ONLY UNTIL YOU *STOLE* IT FROM HIM!

MINA, HONESTLY! YOU'RE FOREVER HARPING ON ABOUT THE *PAST.*

LET'S SEE IF I STILL REMEMBER HOW TO DO THIS...

OH, BLOODY HELL! HANG ON, LANDO! WE'RE COMING!

HMM. WELL, ALL RIGHT...

...BUT ONLY IF YOU JOIN THE PIRATES, TO EVEN THINGS UP.

HAHA! *THIS* IS THE LIFE, EH, YOUNG RAFFLES?

BELIEVE ME, I'VE SWASHED A FEW BUCKLES IN MY TIME.

YES. YES, I'LL BET YOU HAVE...

FOR GOD'S SAKE.

FOR GOD'S BLOODY SAKE...

Jack? BROAD-ARROW JACK? A-AND IS THAT THE *NAUTILUS?* WH-WHAT'S HAPPEN-ING?

BLIMEY! MISS...MURRAY, WAS IT?

CAPTAIN, THIS IS...

I KNOW WHO SHE IS.

I SAW HER ONCE BEFORE WHEN SHE FIRST CAME TO OUR ISLAND FOR MY FATHER.

SHE'S THE WOMAN YOU CAUGHT ON THE BEACH.

BUT...THAT WAS TWELVE YEARS AGO, IN 1898. YOU WOULDN'T HAVE BEEN...

MY GOD.

WERE... WERE YOU THAT LITTLE BABY?

WE WERE ALL BABIES ONCE. AND WE ALL GROW UP.

DO YOU KNOW, MY FATHER HAD NOTHING BUT BAD THINGS TO SAY ABOUT YOU?

HIS FOREMOST COMPLAINT WAS THAT YOU WERE A WOMAN. THIS LEADS ME TO SUPPOSE YOU STRONG AND HONOURABLE.

OTHERWISE, I'D HAVE YOU KILLED.

IF YOU TIRE OF ENGLAND AND FANCY THE PIRATE LIFE, SEND WORD.

UNTIL THEN, LEAVE ME ALONE, AND PERHAPS I'LL LEAVE YOU ALONE.

ALL RIGHT, LOOK LIVELY! RECALL THE RAIDING PARTIES AND SEAL THE HATCHES. WE'RE TAKING HER DOWN.

WAIT! I DON'T EVEN KNOW YOUR NAME...

ME?

I'M NO ONE.

PREPARE TO DIVE, MR. MATE.

Aye-aye, CAPTAIN.

YOU KNOW, ISHMAEL, SHE'S AS BAD AS HER OLD MAN.

HA HA! I'LL TELL YOU WHAT, JACK...

...SHE'S WORSE.

AIN'T IT BLEEDIN' WONDERFUL?

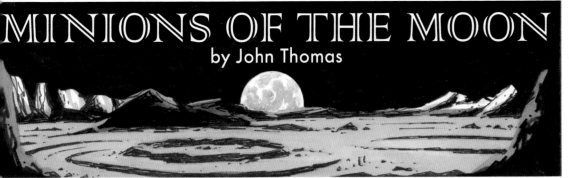

MINIONS OF THE MOON
by John Thomas

(Originally serialised in *Lewd Worlds Science Fiction*, Ed. James Colvin, 183-185, 1969.)

Chapter One: Into The Limbus

*The patient shouts and makes a fuss, is held down
ysically until the sedative they have attempted to re-
e begins to take effect. Eventually the furious invective
rs and slobber drips down onto the restraining-jacket's
oulder. Everything breaks into disconnected words,
ich are dismantled further and reduced to grey, in-
nal fog as consciousness recedes. The patient, by this
int, cannot remember where they are, what year it is,
even their precise identity. The eyes slip out of focus,
ked upon an icy full moon visible through the ward
ndows, or it might be the reflection of a light bulb.*

Bio of Thebes, Abyssinia, 1236 BC:
Love amongst the Troglodytes

The sand a cooling talcum under her bare feet, she
the hunched and grunting elder lead her out by
oonlight from the place where the immortals had
eir stinking burrows, their secluded town of holes
ere in the cloaca of humanity.

Bio had live amongst these sullen creatures for
me four or five years, ever since she'd seen direc-
ns to their settlement carved deep into the rock
rround of that strange pool, not far from Punt, filled
th a blueness that was neither fire nor water. She had
thed there some nights after her escape from Egypt
East Africa upon an expedition, her abrupt departure
ought about by the retraction and eventual inversion
her penis; the enlargement of her breasts. Become a
oman she was beautiful, her salty comrades no more
be trusted, though in this she did not blame them. If
e'd come across such loveliness a little earlier when
e had been a boy, then Bio would have more than
ely raped herself. With this in mind she'd fled west
d had happened on the luminous lagoon of sapphire
asma, had immersed herself in the cold flames of the
dying. On emerging, she had found the stone-etched
agram in the dark by sitting her wet rear upon it as
e dried. Weeks later, following the carven map's in-
uctions, she had come to Abyssinia and the pungent
ttlement of deathless and withdrawn near-animals
no had, like she, swum in the azure mere of light,
t far from Punt, at various remote points in antiquity.
ored, uncommunicative, these unkempt brutes mostly
t sunk in their pits and their own thoughts while they
aited a death that was clearly never going to arrive.

And yet she stayed there with them, chewed roots
d ate grubs with them. She defecated in plain sight as
ey did and held conversations that were for the most

part made of shrugs, sighs, or the raising of a straggly
and trailing brow. The truth was that these torpid and
subhuman demigods amazed her, filled her to the brim
with awe at their solidity, their ancient stillness. They
had the charisma not of men and women but of mountains, timeless features of the human landscape that had
seen vast glaciers come and go, had heard the crash of
fallen stars and stood as witness to uncountable extinc-
tions. In their overpowering scent were untold centuries
of cave-dark copulation, mammoth blood and jungle
murder. Her current companion, said to be amongst the
first of the immortals, was a large and very hairy male
who walked upon his furry knuckle-bones almost as
often as he did his feet. He sniffed and shuffled, leading
her into the Abyssinian night.

He had some days before made her an offer by the
means of gesture: he would show to her a great and
sacred mystery, if she would let him mount her. This
struck her as mythical rather than disagreeable and
thus, with her consent, after a further hour of wading
through sub-lunar silver they arrived at the appointed
place, a desolate expanse of only rocks and fine-milled
sand, where both would satisfy their curiosity.

She kneeled in the blonde pumice and he entered
her, an act of great ferocity that nearly drove the breath
from Bio yet which took but a few seconds to complete,
unlike the man-beast's shuddering climax that went on
and on until her thighs were trickling with primordial
sperm, while both she and her lover howled into the
constellations.

When they had rested, he drew her attention to the
pieces of black stone about them in the white dust.
Upon close inspection these were made from something she had not before encountered, a unique material that seemed to drink light, giving back no glitter
or reflection. Some shards, furthermore, had smoothly
crafted corners. Pinned beneath the detumescent
primitive, she reached out with one hand to touch a
midnight splinter.

Thoughts and images thrummed through her like
a lightning-shock. Pre-human savages at time's dawn
gaping in religious terror at the great square-cut black
stone that stands there in their midst, the bravest creep-
ing hesitantly forth to place a hand upon it. A cascade
of information, fire and numbers, wheels and tools and
weapons. Years later, its unfathomable work completed,
the black block spontaneously shatters and is all but
lost beneath the drifts of aeons…

She let the jet fragment tumble from her hand. Behind her, still inside her, the immortal cupped her face
and lifted it. As though imparting a great secret, first he
pointed to the sharp obsidian chips surrounding their
joined bodies. Then he pointed to the moon.

Mina and Allan, Bloomsbury, 1910:
In the Wake of the Black Nautilus

He found her in their quarters at the museum, in its locked wing. She'd been crying, a release for all the dockside horrors of the afternoon, and when he sat down quietly beside her on their bed at first she shouted at him angrily, then cried some more.

'You didn't talk to her or see her eyes. They were so cold, and she was no more than fifteen years old. What can have happened to her that had killed her girlhood and replaced it with the mantle of her father? It wasn't the heads and slaughter that upset me half so much as that poor child, become a monster before she's become a woman.'

When he placed his arm protectively around her shoulders she at least did not flinch back from him, and they sat there in silence for some moments. He re- flected that they were alone in the museum, in that vast space full of silent, ancient things. Orlando, after all the bloodshed on the wharf, had been much too excited to return to their headquarters and was very likely out carousing in the dives of the East End. Carnacki and the burglar Raffles, both in darker and more sober moods, had each retired home to their separate addresses and their highly individual lives. It was just him and Mina again now.

'Darling, I'm sorry for the mess we made of things with Haddo, and for all the stupid things that Lando said. We acted like a gang of idiots and everything went straight to hell as a result.'

She tilted back her head, and her jade eyes gazed up at him.

'It wasn't your fault. It would all have gone to hell as quickly if we'd done things my way. I was being unfair, blaming you. I think the truth of it is that I'm starting to feel overwhelmed by the enormity of knowing that we're going to live forever, like Orlando, ever since we took our dip in that Ugandan pool. It all seemed like a marvellous lark at first, like something from a fairy story, but just recently the thought of it has come to haunt me. I feel so small, Allan. I feel like I'm standing all alone upon the threshold of eternity. And if it's like this now, what will it be like in a hundred or a thou- sand years?"

He pulled her to him, stroking her black hair to soothe her, and to soothe himself. He knew exactly what she meant, had felt the same sense of unease since stepping from the blue fires of that strange Africa pool and finding himself young again, a strapping fel- low in his early twenties with a lifetime's scars erased or at least most of them. He'd found he still bore the faint signs of injuries sustained in boyhood, and of course the awful marks on Mina's throat had not been wiped away. Perhaps the blue fires had restored them their prime, with any damages they had incurred prio to that point remaining unaffected? Allan didn't know He only knew that he shared his beloved's apprehen- sions of their new immortal state, but had not manage to define those fears as clearly or succinctly as had she He murmured to her and, again, it was as much to rea sure himself as comfort her. About them was the dark the museum, millennia deep.

'I've had the same thoughts, darling, but I prom- ise you, you're not alone. If you're standing upon the threshold of eternity, then I'll be standing there beside you. Mina, you are everything to me. I love you and I promise you I always will.'

Her eyes still brimming, Mina favoured him with a sad smile.

'Always is a bigger word now than it was five years ago, my handsome hero. You may as well promise me the moon.'

He laughed, and gestured out through the tall windows of their bedroom at the bloated silver orb th hung like a Montgolfier balloon in the black heavens south of Oxford Street.

'What, that one? The one shining on the rotting cal bage leaves that choke the gutters along Berwick Stree The one that lights the drunk newspaper-writer's way from the Pillars of Hercules down to the Coach and Horses? Well, if that's the one you want, my love, the you shall have it. Upon my apparently eternal life, I hereby promise you the moon that's over Soho.'

Despite herself Mina was laughing with him now, her vision of the chilly, endless halls of Time beginnin to recede, her dread abating. After all, perhaps Allan was right. Perhaps their love would be enough to out- last empires, outlast worlds. It seemed like long odds but it was at least a ray of hope that she could cling to, bright although remote and distant, like the gib- bous satellite above the boozy brothels of that ancien neighborhood.

Allan and Orlando, Paris, 1964:
Her Long, Adorable Lashes

She lowered her subtly-painted eyes submissively while her demanding lover placed his hand upon her stockinged knee, there in the rear seat of a chauffer- driven limousine as it nosed through the outskirts of th intricately-textured city. It was a new game that they were playing, an experiment intended to enliven their extremely long relationship. Part of the game was that she should not call him by his name, and only speak when she was spoken to. In turn, he would refer to he only by her initial.

They were trying to continue the erotic European odysseys that they had read of in the journals of their 18th-century predecessors, and were travelling at pres ent to a terribly exclusive gentlemen's establishment somewhere amongst the labyrnthine streets. Once

ey'd arrived, her lover would deliver her into a thrill-
gly demeaning form of sexual slavery, to be used and
used by the perverse members as they liked. Know-
g them for descendants of the decadent aristocrats
Silling whom she'd heard her long-dead colleague
rcy Blakeny speak of once, she shivered with a
xture of desire and dread to think of being owned
 them, in that most intimate of manners. Sitting there
side her on the creaking leather rear seat of the car,
 cold against her thighs, her lover turned and spoke,
oving his hand along her sheer hose as he did so.

'It's a shame our mutual ladyfriend decided that
e didn't want to travel with us, isn't it? It's almost as
ough she were making out that she's above this sort
thing, when we both know she isn't. Or at least, she's
t when she's in the right mood, though it's been ages
ice that last occurred. I don't think that it's happened
ice that marvellous long night you showed us in
e Blazing World, when we were just back from the
etched business that surrounded the Black Dossier,
d that was, what, six years ago?'

His hand had by now reached beneath her dress's
m and was exploring at the lace-ensconced and
try delta. She said nothing, but sat trembling with
light as he continued with his deceptively casual
nversation. In the rear-view mirror she could see
eir silent driver's darting eyes as he watched while her
ver fondled her.

'Of course, she's off having her own adventures with
ot of men and women in peculiar costumes, so I
n't expect that ours would interest her. Quite frankly,
on't think her new secret society…"The Seven Stars,"
isn't it called?…sounds half as interesting as the
ternity we're on our way to meet. Speaking of which,
e got a sudden urge to see your bottom, while it still
icially belongs to me. Take off your underthings and
e them to me, as a souvenir.'

Heart hammering, enflamed as much by her own
rem-girl obedience as by the good-looking young
n's deliberately gruff, commanding tone, she did
she was told. The chauffeur's furtive eyes glinted
isciously in the mirror as she lifted up her backside
m the sticky seat and took down the requested items.
impsing her white rear, perfectly round as framed
the black stocking tops, her lover made the obvious
nar comparison. The car drove on and O. sat with
r lovely eyelids lowered, staring at the automobile's
rpeted interior, not daring to look up at him unless he
ked her to.

**ll and Captain Universe, Stardust's Tomb, the Lesser
agellanic Cloud, 1964: Requiem for a Space-Wizard**
The two super-adventurers, of whom but one
s visible, stood framed by the stupendous airlock
eshold of the hollow sun. The Captain, in his rose-
d-primrose uniform, turned to the empty air beside
n with a smile. Thanks to his absolute awareness of
e cosmos, granted by the science-god Galileo, he
uld just make out the otherwise unseen form of his
league standing next to him, the long cloak and the
eird, shadowy helmet of Vull the Invisible picked out
 flickering phosphorescent lines. From this translu-
nt, shimmering mirage it was impossible to draw
y conclusions as to Vull's identity, other than the
pression of a slight and slender man whose age was
determinate. Universe knew his friend to have been

thwarting evil-doers in the early 1930s, long before
the Captain's own career had had its origin, and thus
supposed that his companion must be in his fifties or
his sixties. He clapped one hand on Vull's scrawny,
cape-draped shoulder and asked the blank space for its
opinion of the stunning infra-stellar headquarters that
Captain Universe had taken from another costumed
superman in planet-pulverising mortal combat.

'Well? What do you think? You must admit, it's a
bit roomier than your Star Chamber down beneath
Fitzrovia. The being who constructed it was a demented
megalomaniac, of course, but since I redesigned the
place I rather like it.'

Vull stood silent for a moment and then made reply,
the deep and echoing tones issuing from nowhere with
an almost electronic resonance around the edges of the
sound. Universe wondered, and not for the first time, if
his fellow hero might not be other than human, perhaps
a sophisticated robot or a visitor come from some
distant world.

'It's unbelievable. What are these funny rounded
screens on stalks that seem to sprout from every surface? Are they your additions, or did they come with
the property?'

The Captain, listening carefully to Vull's speech pat-
terns, revised his opinion. The idiosyncrasies betrayed
the speaker as an ordinary human rather than an
android or a spaceman, but suggested that the senior
member of The Seven Stars might be effeminate, which
was to Universe's way of seeing things a more alarming
possibility. Attempting to dispel this thoroughly unwel-
come and surely uncharitable notion, he steered his
invisible companion deeper into the astounding depths
of the star-fortress as he answered.

'No, those are the former occupant's invention.
They're a range of monitors or scanners that enabled
him to view any location in the galaxy, including places
in dimensions other than our own. One of them even
looks into an utterly unheard-of astronomical phenom-
enon, a kind of hole or pocket in the fabric of space-
time itself, inhabited by a grotesque thing that he called
a "Headless Head-hunter." The blighter tried to throw
me into it during our battle, but he wasn't quite as
powerful as he thought he was. I left the view-screens
where they were when I remodelled the remainder
of this artificial star's interior. You never know when
they might come in handy. Anyway, let me guide you
around. I can show you the man himself, if you've a
mind to see him.'

Again, the low, somehow electronic tones emerged
from nothingness.

'I thought you said that he was dead. I thought you
said you'd killed him.'

Leading his unseen guest over gleaming marble
floors between spectacular and self-invented towers of
inscrutable equipment or past huge and cryptic trophies
from his own fantastic exploits, Universe gave an am-
biguous shrug of his broad shoulders.

'It depends on what you mean by dead. You have
to understand that this so-called Space Wizard was
a brutal and sadistic monster. He preferred to punish
adversaries with a fiendishly inventive range of living
deaths, so that they could suffer eternally. I gave the
power-crazed thug a taste of his own medicine, that's all.'

He gestured to the wall-sized portal made from foot-
thick glass that their perambulations had been

leading to. There on the massive window's further side was what appeared to be a chamber filled with an unusually clear and transparent type of ice. Suspended as if floating at its centre was the freakish form of the defeated superman, an almost human entity some eight feet long from head to crown, clad in a skin-tight suit of lurid turquoise. It had far too many ribs and an abnormal musculature, with parts that were wildly disparate in their proportions. The exaggeratedly long head was topped with blonde hair that had frozen into spikes of an unnaturally bright yellow. While Vull stared in silence at the icebound giant, Captain Universe explained as best he could.

'The substance he's encased in is a frozen form of poly-water that he called Ice-9, and he had one or two unfortunates entombed within it when I tracked him back here to this lair for his last stand. I'll swear that he was drunk for that concluding showdown. You could smell the liquor on his breath and he was stumbling and uncoordinated, otherwise I doubt I could have thrown him into his own icy chamber of eternal torment quite as easily as was in fact the case.'

Once more there was a pause before the strange metallic voice made its enquiry.

'What were you fighting over? Were you working under the instruction of your employers at the United Nations?'

Captain Universe looked grim and shook his aubu head.

'The U.N. aren't the only force I answer to. My po ers were given to me by a quintet of science-mystics who've transcended space and time, Pythagoras and Leonardo being counted in that number. These beings exist, along with other awesome presences, upor a level of reality beyond the confines of the mortal realm. Archimedes, Aristotle, and even more recent sub-atomic physicists such as the Swedish theoretica Borghelm. Our friend in the ice-block was attempting to force his way into that sublime elite, and I was give the command to stop him. It's that simple.'

Turning from the eerie exhibit, the pair walked bac across the fake sun's cavernous interior, their conversa tion moving onto other matters.

'Vull, I'm sorry about how The Seven Stars worked out after our one and only victory against the 'Mass. I told my brother Jet about it and he was appalled. That thing might once have been one of his colleagues. Everyone feels bad about what happened.'

Vull, responding, sounded disappointed and yet philosophical.

'I know. I had high hopes for all of us, but now Mars Man and Satin have been forced to drop from sight along with all our other difficulties, I don't think it's possible to put things right. Besides, like you, I'm answerable to higher powers and currently have othe matters to attend to. Could I ask you to return me to our home-world in your spaceship? More specifically need to rendezvous with representatives of the superr forces that I mentioned at a ruined castle in the north Scotland.'

Universe smiled and said he thought that it might arranged.

It was, astonishingly, less than three days later that Vull stood upon the grassy slopes of crumbling Dunbayne Castle, watching for the halo-flash of rippling r diance high in the blue dome of the upper atmospher that would mean Captain Universe's craft had broken the light-barrier and was on its way home towards the distant nebulae. When this had taken place, Vull sat upon the turf and waited for perhaps an hour or more before a wholly different means of transportation drift into view above the northerly horizon. Even from this distance, the invisible adventurer could see the rising pink flecks that were a by-product of the pataphysica ly-constructed vessel's flower-powered engine.

Taking off the helmet of invisibility and startling some nearby sheep by suddenly appearing in their midst, Vull shook her long black hair down to her shoulders and awaited the arrival of the Rose of Nowhe

Prospero and his operatives, the Blazing World, 196 Coming Forth by Day

Over the ornamental root-garden there shone the thousand suns that give this realm its name. The tall and bearded figure in exquisite robes, born to Italian aristocracy some centuries before, peered through the jade and garnet lenses of his pince-nez at the compar assembled on the ageless terraces before him. Four in number, they sat perched upon wide benches carved from single pieces of obsidian that had the staring ey

otif which was the emblem of the Blazing World
aid as a mosic of alabaster. In the star-crammed sky
ove, an Owl-man in a cut silk tunic screeched and
ooped exuberantly.

Seated by herself on the bench closest to the magus
as the marvellously wilful lady music-teacher,
ilhelmina Murray, who had so impressively com-
anded the third incarnation of that league he'd found-
all those years ago. Clad in a single figure-hugging
rment of jet black with cape and leather boots and
ves to match, she sat with an unusual bulb-topped
lmet resting in her lap, gazing attentively at Prospero
ough goggles that had eyes of different colours,
ankly staring discs of red and green.

The three remaining members of the band that the
rmer Duke of Milan had lately summoned sat togeth-
on a separate couch of polished stone. These were
o living wooden dolls named Peg and Sara Jane,
ong with the unnaturally squat and massive figure
o was both their lover and commander. If this star-
ng and yet engaging creature had a given name it was
t known to the magician. Brought here to this daz-
ng fourth-dimensional domain by Queen Olympia
nearby Toyland, the wild-maned black aeronaut had
roduced himself to Prospero as 'a cummun Galley-
g.' From this the wizard had surmised his guest to be
rhaps an escaped slave, come from a hidden cosmos
at was by some means concealed from ordinary
rutiny. That this supposed world and its occupants
re formed from matter of far greater density than
at which made the earthly plane was evidenced by
e fine cracks appearing in the solid block of carved
sidian upon which the extra-terrestrial freebooter
, his thick legs kicking idly, far too short to reach the
ound. Being essentially organic in his nature despite
e discrepancies of his material composition, the dark-
atter buccaneer wore spectacles with mismatched
ses, like Miss Murray. His two literal playthings,
the other hand, were ani-manikins constructed on
e principles established by the late Dr. Copelius and
us did not require the same corrective eyewear. Both
d in short summer dresses that appeared to have
en fashioned from the flag of the United States, the
o impossibly slim wooden figurines sat giggling and
king kittenishly to each other with trilling falsettos in
anguage which the magus recognised as Dutch. The
njuror's assembled crew were clearly growing rest-
s as they waited for him to explain the reason for his
gent summoning. He cleared his throat, and then began.

'No doubt thou wouldst hear why I called thee
nce: what grave calamity requires thine aid. Know
en that this be not an earthly woe, but, rather, it af-
cts another sphere.'

Prospero gestured with one ring-decked hand, heavy
th chryosprase and tourmaline, and in the air before
em there appeared a vision of an unmistakable pale
o against a field of sequinned night. The Galley-wag
ed his huge head quizzically.

**'By the great quim o' singularity! Be that not
ur whirl's loon-lamp?'**

The elderly mage and young music teacher felt
much as heard the creature's voice, with its inhu-
anly low register reverberating in their bellies and
e marrow of their bones. Prospero nodded and, with
e extended fingertip, touched the diaphanous and
immering image in some half-a-dozen places, leaving
ed dot of pulsing phosphorescence at each point of
ntact.

'Aye, ebon navigator of the void, it is the moon I
conjure to plain sight. There, marked in crimson, see
Earth's colonies, where fly the stiff and windless flags
of France, of England, Germany, America. Yet are there
conflicts in those cratered lands that are not born of
earthly enmities. Two species native to that silv'ry ball
have lately clashed together in a war which, ranging far
across the lunar globe, endangers the terrestrial settle-
ments. I fear that if these battles should persist, Earth's
settlers shall be forced to relocate unto a certain area of
that sphere where we wouldst rather that they ventured
not, not until it is the appointed time there at the dawn
of a new century. I charge thee to set sail, then, for
night's jewel, there to placate these warring lunar tribes
that our Blazing World's schemes go not awry.'

Miss Murray raised one black-gloved hand, and
Prospero permitted her to speak.

'Most noble Duke, might I ask why my colleagues
Allan and Orlando were not summoned to this meeting? Are they not to journey with us?'

The enchanter shook his head. Across the terraces,
a sun that had a wry and sleepy smile was setting over
diamond quays and ululating minarets.

'They undertake an amorous idyll in Europe's dens
of pain and ecstasy, unwilling or unable to respond to
all my imprecations and demands. I fear I know my former squire of old, lascivious and truant in her way, and
hazard we shall see no more of her nor of thy youthful
huntsman paramour until their lusty chase hath run its
course.'

The music teacher, rising from her bench, pursed her
lips disapprovingly.

'I see. Then we may as well board the Rose of Nowhere and make ready to embark as soon as possible. I
bid you a good aeon, Prince of Necromancers.'

Prospero watched as the odd quartet walked off
across the ornamental gardens, with the Galley-wag
leaving behind him webs of crack and fracture on the
paving stones in lieu of footprints. The twin doll-girls
held hands as they skipped together with their flag-
skirts flaring, chattering excitedly in Dutch, and only
Wilhelmina Murray seemed disheartened. With her
long cloak trailing mournfully and the outlandish
helmet underneath her arm she strode away between
fantastic topiaries. The magician gestured, and the evo-
cation of the moon floating beside him fell apart into
a billion scintillating motes. Chewing the ends of his
moustache, he hoped that this was not an omen.

Mina and the Galley-wag, the Rose of Nowhere, 1964: Huckleberry Friends

Wearing the borrowed costume of a long-deceased Vull the Invisible she stood there on the deck, gripping the rail and marvelling that she could still respire although their boat had sailed beyond the thinnest reaches of Earth's upper atmosphere some half an hour before. Admittedly the air she breathed was scented heavily with roses, a by-product of the craft's unusual method of propulsion, but this was scarcely a hardship.

Behind them, her home planet was a stupefying opal while ahead was an infinity of ink where countless flakes of furnace-light hung in suspension. Somewhere down below, in the beguiling swirl and mottle of the blue world's cloud and ocean, she knew that her friends pursued their earthly lives as usual. Fathoms beneath the great sprawl of the sea, an ageing savage beauty known as Jenny Nemo would be lighting candles at the starboard shrine of her night-black submersible in memory of her late husband, the dependable Broad-Arrow Jack. Elsewhere within the seabed-grazing vessel, Jenny's daughter Hira would still be asleep in the next cabin to her own child, Jenny's grandson. Not yet six, Jack Dakkar was the fruit of an arranged dynastic union between his mother and the since-deceased air-pirate Armand Robur, a descendant of the more notorious Jean. Much as she'd liked the little boy when they had met, Mina could not help thinking that he represented a potentially explosive mix of lethal bloodstocks.

Then, of course, there were her other comrades. There was witty and ingenious Queen Olympia with her brooding consort in the snow-surrounded pocket of eternal summer known as Toyland. At their various secret bases or their alias day-jobs there were Captain Universe and the few other super-people who where left from Mina's recent incognito and foredoomed attempt to form a band of champions, while somewhere in the demimonde of Paris were her lovers, Allan and the pulchritudinous Orlando, hurling themselves into a debauch in an attempt to dull the dread that came with immortality.

Her reverie was interrupted by a doleful and protesting creak from the ship's black-material timbers, somewhere close behind her. Turning, Mina found herself confronted by the Galley-wag. Like her, he had dispensed with the two-coloured spectacles now that they were no longer in the 4-D territories of the Blazing World, and the white saucers of his lidless eyes shone from the unreflective dark globe of his shaggy head as he addressed her formally, according to his own conventions.

'Bread and tits, resplendent swan of Peril! Does yer bezoms heave fer home?'

The subterranean pitch of his inhuman voice made the dark metal of the handrail hum in resonance. Mina smiled fondly as she ventured a reply in the same idiom.

'Bread and tits to *you,* brave rider on the night's starry pudendum. No, I wasn't homesick. I was thinking about all the people that we're leaving back on Earth, behind us. I suppose that I was feeling a bit…oh! I say, what's that, just off the port bow?'

The ethereal mariner swivelled his massive cranium to peer in the direction she had indicated. Mina noticed, quite irrelevantly, that he had a bottle tucked into the red sash of his belt. She fleetingly supposed this to be rum of an unworldly distillation. Something glittering approached them, tumbling through trans-planetary gloom and coruscating as it came, as though lit by its own internal fire.

'Why, by my tripes! It books to be a lantern-cadaver encubed in frusticles!'

As the trajectory of the revolving and illuminated mass began to take it under the ascending Rose of Nowhere, Mina gasped. It was a lump of ice, and at its heart was a contorted, black-clad corpse still clinging to a ball of greenish radiance. As the refrigerated mass rotated she found herself gazing into the eternally-unblinking, horror-stricken eyes of her late adversary, the depraved professor of mathematics, spymaster and criminal, James Moriarty. His gaunt features, locked in a last breathless scream, were under-lit by the crepuscular glow of the Cavorite clutched to his frozen breast. Then the corpse-satellite was gone, fallen away beneath their vessel to continue its unending orbit.

Hesitantly, still stunned by this unexpected meeting with her former foe, Mina communicated what she knew of the dead, icebound figure to her host. The Galley-wag gave a low, sympathetic growl that fractured a glass dial in his array of instruments.

'He sounds to be a noxic vile-guard, an' yer whirl's well rid o' hum. Now, wishin' no intrudence, I'd stamped herewards to bequire if you were wantin' blanket-company amid this wendless vastard of a night? I know as Sarey-Jane's taken a varnish to yer since you lost yer blondery, if you were in a mood fer sallymappin'. Alsewise, yer'd be wellcum bunked betwixt me an' the twin of 'um.'

Realising that she'd been politely propositioned and belatedly identifying the glass bottle jutting from the Galley-wag's red sash as being filled with linseed oil rather than an exotic rum, Mina felt both obscurely flattered and amused as she respectfully declined his invitation. Taking no offence, the baryonic buccaneer returned below decks to his greased and squeaking love-toys, leaving Mina with her thoughts and the indifferent canopy of stars. Ahead of them, beyond the Rose of Nowhere's shark-faced prow, a golf-ball moon inflated steadily across the next few hours until it filled the firmament from rim to rim.

– To Be Continued –

The Real Deal